RESTRICTED WATERS

KARA LYNN CONYER

Waterhouse Books

ISBN: 978-0-9899237-05
ISBN-10: 0989923703
Published October 2013

For Judy Britt

.

CHAPTER 1

I WOKE UP THIS MORNING TO THE KIND OF WET, DISMAL snow that can only fall in early spring. The kind that creeps inside your bones and insists winter will never leave. It was so deep inside me that, even though I knew where I was going, even though I had been packing for weeks, I just had to cram my warm slippers into the corner of my duffel bag before running out the door. It's not that I didn't know they would be useless on a dive boat in the Caribbean. It's just that I have a hard time accepting the idea that the world around me can change so dramatically in just a few short hours.

Even now that I'm here in Florida, standing alone under the searing tropical sun, something inside me rejects the fact that this is the same sun still hanging in the sky back home behind a blanket of cold winter clouds. My hair, dull and frizzy when I left New England this morning is steaming into shiny, brown ringlets that stick to the back of my neck and along the sides of my face.

The shocking heat is nothing compared to the view in front of me. The shipyard is piled high with boats, all of them caked with the Fouling, a stony black crust that looks like concrete. The few boats left in the water are listing sluggishly to the side. They are heavy with the Fouling—massive colonies of tiny organisms that spread under water and cover the boats like concrete tumors. It weighs them down as it grows until the water eventually swallows them whole. Scenes like this have been all over the news for months. From here to Virginia, coastal towns have been devastated. Fishing, shipping, tourism, everything shut down. But what the news could not show was the silence, the still feeling of death and abandon. Hundreds of thousands of people have left their homes and moved north or west to look for work. They've lost everything. This silence is what's left behind.

Scanning this graveyard of a marina, I finally spot them at the head of a long pier: Dr. Candace Warren and two men I haven't met yet. I'm so relieved to see people, I have to remind myself to walk, not run, toward them. Dr. Warren is known around the world for her groundbreaking work in marine ecology, and I have met her exactly twice. Each time I found her intimidating, even without the reputation. She made it clear she is all business, and she has no patience for novices. She looks a little softer now, but only slightly, in her crisp white shorts and a bright tropical scarf tied tightly around her short hair. Her dark-coffee skin has more gold in it here than it had up north.

I straighten my shoulders beneath the load of my bags and try not to look sixteen.

"You made it," Dr. Warren says without looking up from her clipboard. I plop down my duffel bag, but before I can take off my backpack, she gives me a quick introduction.

Dr. Dirk Peterson is tall, with short, wavy hair and large square shoulders that look uncomfortably stuffed into his dark blue polo. When he shakes my hand, he looks directly at my eyes, gives an extra little pump, and says, "Dr. Peterson, NOISI. You can call me Dirk." He means he's from the National Oceanographic Invasive Species Institute. He almost looks too young to be an expert, but everything about him is serious. A little too serious.

"Alannis Summers," I say nodding back at him.

The other guy, Dr. Guillermo Marino, seems a little friendlier in his beige shirt with green palm fronds and bright red birds on it. His round face sits right on top of his shoulders without a neck between them. His sandy brown hair is stick-straight and streaked with grey. It hangs loosely over his eyebrows, stopping just short of two bright green eyes. Dr. Warren tells me he is her counterpart from the Latin American Institute for Scientific Research. He must be our Cubbarros guide. He takes my hand softly and says in a thick accent, "It's a pleasure."

Introductions over, they turn immediately back to sorting gear. Piles of scuba equipment, cameras, and black and yellow waterproof cases filled with who knows what. I'm standing here pitched forward with my shoulders hunched around the straps of my heavy backpack like a little kid waiting at the bus stop.

Dr. Warren waves her hand toward the dock. "We're the last boat," she says. "On the end. Go put your stuff down and come back to help load." Walking down the long dock, I refuse to look at the half sunken, abandoned boats on either side of me. They are just dominoes falling one by one to the sandy bottom. I want to trust that Dr. Warren has a plan for avoiding their fate.

Last fall, distress calls began coming from boats in the Caribbean and the Gulf of Mexico, their gear so jammed with the Fouling that they were dead in the water. By February, there were more drifting ships than tugs to rescue them. The Fouling built up so quickly on their hulls that the weight of it pulled many of them to the bottom of the ocean. They say it sank an entire fleet of oil tankers in three days.

When I find our boat, it's bigger than I expected, about 90 feet long with a wheel house and two covered decks. The main deck level looks roomy with large windows and a sliding glass door facing the back of the boat. It opens to the after deck where we'll be staging our dives. There's a row of portholes below the rub rail. That must be where the sleeping cabins are.

Her name, *Sun Joule*, is painted in white against the dark blue stern. As I get closer, I notice the guy standing on deck. My eyes sting from the sweat rolling off my forehead, but I see that he's not much older than me. He has that blond-haired, blue-eyed, summer-sports model kind of look that makes me think everything out of his mouth is going to be followed by the words dude, or bro, or even worse, brah.

"Welcome aboard," he says, reaching for my duffel bag with a broad smile.

He takes my duffel in one hand, and holds out the other to help me onto the boat as if I were a clumsy landlubber. I hook my thumbs in the straps of my backpack and step on by myself—I don't need coddling. I'm here to work. "Thanks." I say and slip past him as I take back my duffel.

"Right this way," he chirps brightly, and I follow him to the door amidships. "You're Alannis, right?" He sounds like a tour guide. Like he thinks I'm here on a field trip or something.

Cool air hits me the second we enter the main cabin. I'm soaked, and all I can think about is a cold drink and a shower. I haven't answered his question yet, but the guy doesn't seem to be waiting for one as he walks over to the galley and reaches into the fridge. When he pops up with a Coke and a water in his hand, I understand both his age and his tour-guide welcome. He's not a part of the scientific team. A logo on his shirt pocket says "*MV Sun Joule*" in blue letters that match his board shorts. "Jake" and the words "First Mate" are embroidered beneath the logo. Jake extends the drinks toward me. The water bottle is sweating as profusely as I am.

"Thanks," I say again between long gulps.

"Let me show you below." He leaves my duffel bag in the middle of the salon for me to carry. I'm glad he got the message. Down the stairs, my cabin is the second on the left. "You're sharing with Lacey," he says.

That's when the bony elbow of an older girl with a white-blonde ponytail and lobster-red shoulders rams right into my chest. This, I learn through some awkward apologies on both sides, is Lacey, Dr. Warren's new assistant. She must have spun out of the cabin across from us. There's a guy in there stacking boxes on the top bunk. Lacey looks like she could be about twenty-five or so, but I'm not sure. She's in a hurry to help load, and so am I. The sooner we get away from this place and into open water, the better.

All the rushing around is wasted, though. There's some delay surrounding the navigational charts—the maps we'll follow to find our research sites. Ordinarily, you can just buy charts at a marine store, or download them right into the boat's GPS navigation system. But we'll be working around the Cubbarros Islands. Restricted waters where satellite signals are blocked and no one has been allowed to go for more than fifty years. Dr. Warren knew the Commission would wait until the last minute to give us the charts and clear the satellite transmissions, but no one expected it to take this long.

When we finally pull away from the marina I stand on the lower deck, trying to see over the side. I want to know if she is riding low in the water, a sign the Fouling has begun to cake the bottom of the boat. I listen for a strain on the engine, but oddly, there is only the sound of waves slapping the hull as it slices through the water. On our way out of the harbor, there is no place to look where I can avoid the awful devastation. All along the waterfront, marinas, piers, docks—everything is encrusted with the Fouling. I go below, hoping it won't take long to reach open water. Away from the land and all this disgusting blackness.

Not long after the land has disappeared from sight, Jake calls us to the upper deck for a briefing. Captain Jerry Sullivan introduces himself and tells us he goes by Sully. He's a retired engineer from the navy, and he built this boat himself. His white hat keeps the sun off his head, but the shiny black visor and nautical rope knot on the front of it make me smile. It's not an official hat, just the kind of hat yacht captains wear when they want everyone to know who they are. When I was little, my mom and I called that a scrambled egg hat because of the way the yellow rope looks like scrambled eggs from a distance. Captain Sully is telling us about the boat, why it's different from the boats that are piled like corpses in the Marina.

"She's the only solar-electric boat in the world right now," he beams. "Even the navy doesn't have anything like this yet. Those panels on the very top. . . solar. That paint there on deck," Sully spreads his arms out wide for emphasis, "all solar." He taps the rail with each word as he says, "State. Of. The. Art. Even the paint on the hull collects sunlight reflected off the water. No oil, no gas. The Fouling won't touch it."

The Fouling started right after the big oil spill last year, and scientists think it eats petroleum and petroleum products like gasoline and plastic. It seems to have followed the spill up the coastline. Now it eats anything with the slightest bit of oil or plastic on it.

The guy I saw stacking boxes in the cabin across from mine clears his throat. He's tall and kind of soft in the middle with short, curly, red hair and doughy white skin. He looks at Captain Sully and says, "Has this boat been in the water the whole time? Since it started?"

"No." Captain Sully takes his hat off and smoothes a couple strands of white hair down across his otherwise bare scalp. He stares at him as if trying to remember something. "It's Matt isn't it?"

"Yeah, that's right. I was just wondering if the boat's been in the water here with the Fouling for any length of time."

"We just put her in yesterday," Sully says. "After the Fouling started, we ran her for a long time, but when the dive business crashed, we didn't see the sense of leaving her in the water. Why tempt it, right?"

Sully knows we're all wondering the same thing Matt's wondering. How he can be so sure the Fouling won't touch us. "We stayed pretty clean while we were in, though," he goes on. "Jakey dove in every day to check her hulls and scrub her down." I flash a glance at Jake who seems to flinch when Sully calls him Jakey. All of a sudden, the resemblance is clear. Captain Sully is his father. "Our hulls were getting that early slime on them," Sully continues. "Just the beginning of the Fouling, but it didn't seem to take hold, and Jakey was keeping up with it pretty good. We're pretty sure we've got the advantage here."

"Pretty sure" isn't very reassuring. Neither is the fact that everyone seems anxious to get out of the harbor that was so dense with the Fouling.

Sully tells us that when the sun sets, we'll be able to run for most of the night on battery power. Then we'll anchor and start up again with the sun in the morning. Until then, he says, no electric usage, no lights, no computers, nothing until tomorrow. That doesn't bother me until he says we'll have no internet for the whole trip. There's a satellite link, but it's for the navigation station and emergency sat phone only. Really? I expected to at least be able to text my friends. Felicia was going to send me updates and pics of anything important. I'm supposed to be her *what not to wear to the prom* consultant. Now, I really am going to miss the rest of my junior year.

When Sully finishes, he turns to Dirk who has been standing against the rail with his big arms crossed tightly in front of him and one ankle crossed over the other. Dirk steps up to give us a rundown on the dive planning. He says he's got extra everything, and he's trained to repair and rebuild all of our equipment. "I take safety very seriously," he says, puffing out his big chest. "Now, I know I'm not the most senior scientist onboard, but if you don't mind, Candace, I'd like to keep tabs on everyone's logs and dive computers, too." I think he has just appointed himself dive master for the trip. Candace raises her eyebrows and then just shrugs her shoulders as if to say, "Whatever."

Jake steps up and tells us lunch will be ready in about 30 minutes.

It's the kind of lunch I could get used to. Garlic bread, shrimp and salad. As we eat, the scientists compare notes about their work on invasive species around the world. The casual way they fill their plates in the galley and settle into the long bench seats around the settee makes it obvious they've all done this before—boarded a boat with colleagues and set out for a couple months of diving and working. Until now, the idea of being away from home, living with working scientists—strangers—for weeks on end was one of the most exciting prospects of my fantasy-job-come-true. Now, with nothing to add to the conversation, I'm a little uneasy about finding a way to fit in.

I skewer a perfectly cooked shrimp with my fork and wonder if, back home, my brother Alex will claim my seat at the dinner table tonight. He prefers my window view of the back yard over his usual view of the kitchen. It's a ridiculous thing to think about, but my mind is wandering all over the place. I'll be more comfortable once we start diving and concentrating on the work. I've been SCUBA diving almost every weekend since I was twelve, and I can do whatever they need me to do underwater. Once we start working, I won't be just an add-on. I'll be a part of the team.

*

I hold on to that thought after lunch, carrying it with me to the upper deck where I spend the afternoon alone watching the endless blue ocean pass beneath us. Dinner is mostly the same, filled with conversation about interesting lives and exciting careers. For the most part, I just listen. After dinner, Lacey and I unpack our clothes in the small space of our shared cabin, an uncomfortable thing in front of someone you just met. I feel the heat coming off her sunburned shoulders as she tosses bikinis and lacy things across her bunk in front of us. I'm not sure if there is a method to this, or how she plans to stuff them all into her locker next to the vanity, but that's her thing.

I keep my hands working close to my body as I fold my collection of board shorts and camis. I stack them neatly on one corner of my mattress before transferring them into my locker. Lacey doesn't seem to notice that I'm trying to keep a respectful distance between our things. She doesn't seem to appreciate that I didn't even question her claim on the bottom berth. She just assumed I would take the tiny upper one that's half the size of a single bed. She is much more interested in grilling me for information about how I got here.

"So, are you a student at Braverton or something?"

"No, but I will be going there for marine biology." I hope I can avoid telling her I'm only a junior in high school.

"So, what, are you like on some kind of advanced study program?"

"Not really, I just went to Dr. Warren and volunteered to be her intern." I figure Dr. Warren already told everyone my dad is the dean of the University, and her boss. Lacey just wants to hear me say it. I'm sure she thinks that's why I'm here, but my dad didn't even know about it at first. In fact, it took a lot of work to convince him and my school principal that this is like being a foreign exchange student. Except instead of going to Europe, I'll be doing science.

"Well, you should feel lucky. It's not every kid who gets to go on a research cruise to Cubbarros with a famous scientist and a secret agent from the Commission."

Agent? She sees the surprise on my face and smiles. "Dirk, can't you tell?" That's when I feel the boat slow. Swiftly moving feet thump on deck, and someone yells. We drop our clothes and run outside.

Guillermo stands at the rail just outside the doorway, smoking a cigar and looking at the sky as if nothing is happening. "Ah, the Milky Way, it's so beautiful." Jake is up at the bow calling something to Captain Sully in the wheelhouse. Dirk flies past us and leaps up the stairs to the second deck.

Dr. Warren calls through the doorway behind us, "What's going on, Guillermo?"

"I don't know. I was just enjoying the evening." His calm voice sounds almost lyrical. "We should maybe sit back here. Stay out of the way until they settle it." He leads Lacey and me to the back deck where all the dive gear is, but Dr. Warren heads straight up the stairs. That's when a green flash catches my eye and zips out of sight like underwater lightning.

I run to the rail; green and white flashes dart back and forth under and around the boat. I can't tell how deep they are, but they're big. Eight, ten feet. Maybe more. I've never seen anything like this. I'm familiar with the bioluminescent creatures in New England, but those are small—tiny plankton and fist sized jellies. They sparkle just beneath the surface, and light up like glow sticks when waves or big fish disturb them. A big fish can leave long streaks of light through the water, but this is something completely different.

"Come look, what is this?" I call over to Lacey and Guillermo.

"Oh my god. They're beautiful," Lacey gasps.

"Squid." Guillermo glances quickly over the side with disinterest.

"It can't be, they're HUGE!" Lacey says.

"Yes, they are like squid," he says. "Do not stand close. They will jump from the water and carry a man overboard. Very dangerous."

Guillermo will not look over the side. He puts his hands on our shoulders to lead us away from the rail. His snuffed out cigar dangles from his fingers right next to my face. I tilt my head away from his hand, trying to dodge the bitter smell of burnt tobacco. "Soon, the Pleiades will rise," he says shifting his gaze to the sky. "Do you know these stars?" Lacey and I are too fascinated to look up. Whatever they are, there are many of them. I just want one to come to the surface so we can see what it is. Giant squid are supposed to be rare in the tropics. Just then, the boat slows to an idle. The lights streak away and are gone.

I dash forward thinking maybe I'll see them from the bow. Dirk stands in the middle of the side deck next to the main cabin. He's blocking my way. "Did you see them?" I ask.

"What?" he says.

"The fish, or squid, or whatever. They were huge bioluminescent flashes all around."

"No," he says sternly, moving toward me so I have no choice but to turn around and go back to the aft deck.

On my way there, Jake comes flying down the stairs and almost runs into me. "I'm setting the anchor," he says to us. "I need everyone inside. We're off course in the blackout zone, and our navigation is down."

CHAPTER 2

DR. WARREN IS RIGHT BEHIND US WHEN WE HEAD INSIDE. "Dr. Warren, did you see those things?" I gasp. "Were they squid?"

She looks annoyed. "It's Candace. Please." She told me to call her Candace at dinner, but I'll have to try hard to think of her that way. The pinched look on her face tells me I'm not getting an answer about the squid, and I should be more concerned about our situation. We stand in the middle of the salon. Blue-cushioned bench seats line the walls on either side of the room, but no one sits. It's as if we're frozen outside a school during a fire drill, waiting for someone to tell us what to do.

"What are they saying on the bridge?" Guillermo asks Candace.

"It's the charts," she answers. "They might not be compatible with the GPS software. After all that trouble, you would think they'd give us the right charts, wouldn't you?"

"Do we know where we are?" Guillermo asks.

"We don't." Her voice is stiff, suppressing anger. "By the charts, we're some 100 miles from the Cubbarros. But both global positioning systems put us much closer, somewhere in the middle of the blackout zone." We're exactly where the Commission doesn't want us to be.

Dirk cuts Candace off in a booming voice before he even enters the salon. "OK. I need everyone to stay inside until we straighten this thing out. The Commission knows why we're here. It's not our fault. It's all good."

Lacey throws me a look that practically screams, "See, I told you!"

I hope he's right.

The Commission doesn't admit to it, but everyone knows they sink ships that wander into restricted waters near the Cubbarros Islands. A few years ago, an entire navy fleet disappeared out here. A Commission spokesperson told reporters they were doing their best to find them, but nothing was ever found. No wreckage, no floating debris, no bodies, nothing. Everyone knows, Navy fleets don't just disappear.

The only reason we have permission to be here at all is that Dr. Warren thinks there may be something here to help stop the Fouling. When the Commission gave us the charts, they left large areas blank and made it clear that those waters remain strictly off limits—the black-out zones. And just to be sure we don't stray, they've installed a transponder on our antennae so they can track our location at all times. She claps her hands together and points us all to the companionway stairs that lead to our cabins below. "Well, there it is then," she says, "I'm sure we'll have this sorted out by morning."

With perfect mistiming, Matt—the soft, doughy guy from the debriefing—lumbers up the companionway into the salon. I learned during dinner that he was Candace's head research technician at her previous lab. He looks completely surprised to see us all standing there.

"Are we having a meeting?" You've got to be kidding me. He's been below this whole time. When he mounts the last step to join us in the salon, we're ready to go to our cabins.

"Come on, Matt," Candace stands in front of him, forcing him to turn around and walk back down the stairs. "We're anchoring for the night." As I open the door to my cabin, I see Guillermo put his wretched cigar back between his teeth and head up the stairs. I suppose he doesn't intend to miss a smoke beneath the Pleiades.

Lacey and I return to unpacking, but I keep looking out the porthole, wondering if we'll see those flashing animals again. "You don't think they're squid, do you?" I ask her.

"Those things? No way. We had squid off the coast of California, and those are definitely not squid."

"Do you really think they're dangerous?"

"I don't know, Guillermo thinks they are, but he is from Cubbarros." Which means he's just superstitious. Cubbarros is a chain of islands that form a roughly triangular-shape in the middle of the Caribbean Sea. The whole area has come to be known as the Cubbarros Triad. Before the Commission took over, the Triad was shrouded in myths about sea monsters, disappearing ships, even magnetic fields that transport people to alien worlds. Some tried to say the missing Navy ships were another Triad mystery, but most people don't take the whole supernatural thing seriously. Except for those who grew up on Cubbarros. They still hold on to the legends from their childhoods about dangerous creatures and mysterious things that happen in the water.

"When were you in California?" I ask her.

"I went to University of California in San Diego. That's where I got my PhD." It shouldn't surprise me that she has her doctorate, but it does. I see Lacey more like one of the college students who lived with us when I was growing up. My parents called them "au pairs," but they were mostly just students who couldn't afford housing. They got paid to live with us and hang out with Alex and me after school. They made dinner and drove us around when my mother traveled for work.

Doctor Lacey Something scoops up her separate piles of clothing and dumps them into two drawers. What was the point of folding? "I study biological controls," she says, "you know, natural things that help increase or limit the population of certain species."

She holds up an impossibly tiny bikini that, on first glance, I mistake for a headband with bows. She looks at the strip of fabric, "I probably should have left some of this stuff at home."

My duffel bag is nearly empty, but I pull out the thick, fuzzy slippers I've been hiding. I hold them up next to her bikini. "Me too!" Our laughter breaks the tension, but my uneasiness doesn't really go away.

When I finally climb into my bunk, the lapping of water against the hull reverberates through the cabin. It is the only sound. In my dreams, those animals fly above us wearing Commission uniforms, while the Fouling crawls up the sides of the boat like the tentacles of a giant squid. Pulling us down into the sea.

I wake up to darkness and the rhythm of the boat swinging gently on its anchor. Slowly, a faint glow spills through the porthole next to me and lands across my arms. The sun is still far from rising, but a pale yellow sliver appears on the horizon. We have made it through the night without sinking, or being sunk. I slither down from my bunk, careful not to wake Lacey.

The air outside is sweet and salty. The pre-dawn sky, full of warmth and energy, washes away last night's anxieties. I love this time of day. There is no sign of land in the distance, and the water looks deep and warm. I can't even explain why, but if you know the cold winter waters up north, you'd know just by looking at it that this water's warm. It's so still and peaceful. I inhale a deep breath of Caribbean air. The urge to jump in is almost overwhelming, but I settle for sitting on the swim platform with my feet dangling in the water.

It's crystal clear, and my feet appear to ripple below the surface. The longer I sit here watching them, the more I wonder what's down there. Is the bottom covered in Fouling? All of a sudden, it occurs to me that the hull has not been checked. Last night, we anchored, and no one went in to see if the Fouling has started to grow on the bottom of the boat.

Maybe I should get up and tell someone. Knock on Sully's door and ask him to inspect the hull. What if he won't? What if he's insulted that I questioned his perfect "state-of-the-art" boat?

The sky is beginning to brighten, and the others will be up soon, but I have to check. I want to see it for myself. I grab a mask and fins, ease myself quietly into the water, and sink in over my head. The water feels wonderful, warm and salty. I circle the boat, careful not to make a sound. From what I can see the hull looks clean. Diving under, I slide my hand along the boat. I think I feel a thin coat of slime. That's the way the Fouling starts, a thin colony of gelatinous single celled organisms that eventually eat into the surface until it has a good grip. Then it begins to build the crust around itself. I wipe the hull more purposefully, but nothing comes off on my hand.

Off the bow, something clings to the anchor chain. I pull myself down to get a better view. As it comes into focus it resembles a head of wilted lettuce strung on a flag pole. It's just seaweed waving in the current. Then a shadowy figure darts beneath me. My heart jumps. I strain to see into the distance. There's something large. A wall. No, more like a peaked tower. Whatever it is, I can't see it well. It's far away and everything is monochromatic and hazy in the pre-dawn light. I can't swim to it either. My lungs ache for air.

I surface on the boat's starboard side, the right side when you're on deck facing the bow. A loud "Psssst" sound comes from somewhere above me. Jake leans over the rail, waving his hands furiously. "Get out of there, what do you think you're doing?" He's whispering so loud I wonder why he bothers. When I get to the dive platform, he's back there, ready to grab me right out of the water.

His reaction seems a little over the top. "I was checking the hull," I call out more quietly than he did.

"What are you trying to do? We're not supposed to be here."

"I'm not trying to do anything," Does he think I'm stupid? "I just wanted to see if there was Fouling."

He takes a deep breath, tightens his jaw and looks around nervously. "Well?"

I shake my head no. Jake bends down until his face is almost level with mine in the water. "Alannis, Get out. Now. Get back on the boat."

Of course, I know it would be a good idea to get out, but something else inside me enjoys seeing him so frantic. "You should come in for just a second," I say. Besides, I want to go back and see what's down there.

"Are you crazy?"

"I mean it," I insist. He stands up and looks back at the empty deck. I don't mean to be mean, but now that I'm pushing his buttons, I can't seem to stop. "Shouldn't this be your job? Checking the boat? Just come look for a second, and I'll get out." I swim a couple of feet away, and he watches me for a few seconds as if deciding what to do.

Then he tiptoes up to the gear rack and grabs a mask and

fins. Back on the platform he pleads one more time, "Come on, get in the boat."

"Come in the water, and I will. I promise."

He nearly rips his shirt off and yanks on the fins. As he pulls his mask down over his eyes, I round the stern and swim as fast as I can toward the bow. Jake catches up quickly. So, I suck in a big gulp of air and dive below. Hand over hand I pull myself down the anchor chain. The bottom looks to be about 40 feet below the boat. In the distance, a drop-off leads into deeper water. I'm about 20 feet down when Jake catches up. He grabs my fin to stop me. He tugs, but I pull my foot away from his loose grip. I look back to see him pulling himself quickly down the anchor chain toward me. He sees it, too. Just past the drop-off a massive, dark silhouette. It's out of focus and dim, but the outline is distinct. It looks like the bow of an enormous ship reaching straight up out of the deep. Jake grabs my arm and pulls me hard to the surface. I can't hold my breath any longer, so I don't put up a fight.

"Did you see that?" I say as soon as we break the surface.

"Shhh, be quiet," he says.

"Jake, it was huge."

"Alannis, we didn't just see that. I told you, we're not supposed to be here."

I'm about to dive back down when he grabs my waist and pulls me toward him as if he's going to kiss me. It happens so quickly, I don't have a chance to react. When our faces are inches apart, his eyes lock onto mine, and they're not kissing eyes. They're panicked eyes. "Laugh," he hisses through gritted teeth.

I'm about to push him away and yell things at him that I don't think I've ever said out loud when I notice Dirk over Jake's shoulder. He is on the bow in a wide stance with his fists jammed onto his hips.

"Don't look at him," Jake whispers, "act like you're having fun." He strikes a pretty boy smile and laughs as if he were in a Coke commercial. I try to make a natural laughing sound, but it feels stupid. He pulls me closer. "We didn't see anything," he whispers. "Nothing." Anger has replaced his panic, and his rough hands feel unfamiliar and awkward against my skin. Jake turns around as if he's going to dive under, but then he stops. "Oh, Dirk, hi," he calls in mock surprise. "Nice morning, huh?"

Dirk says nothing. He doesn't move. With the dawn light behind him, he casts a long menacing shadow toward us. Suddenly, I feel the weight of the secret between Jake and me. Maybe Lacey is right about Dirk being an agent. Walking silently along the side of the boat, he follows us as we swim to the dive platform. I'm feeling a little panic now myself. We both swim as fast as we can and climb quickly aboard.

"What the hell do you kids think you're doing in there? This isn't a vacation," he growls. That was stupid of me. Really, really stupid. Why didn't I just get out when Jake asked me to? What was I trying to prove? If the Commission sent that ship to the bottom, the last thing they want is for someone to find it.

We scramble onto the boat, and Dirk stomps back inside shaking his head. Jake hangs up his mask and fins, and rushes up the stairs to the second deck before I have a chance to say anything.

CHAPTER 3

IT TAKES HALF THE DAY FOR SULLY TO GET THE CHARTS working properly with the GPS and the navigation gear. I spend most of that time reading in my cabin, preoccupied with what Jake and I saw. A hundred pages into one of the books I packed, I still have no clue what it's about. I shouldn't have been swimming this morning, but I can't help but wonder if that enormous dark pillar below us is a ship. It's still sitting there undiscovered just beyond the drop off. I've dived on dozens of shipwrecks back home, and I've always imagined discovering a wreck no one has ever seen.

Light spills into the cabin through the porthole and sweeps across the pages of my book. We're turning. I'm so distracted, even the clang of the anchor chain winding onto the windlass hadn't registered until now. The solar engines are silent, and only when we begin to move forward does it sink in. We're leaving. I will never know what that place was.

*

Soon after we get underway I find Jake in the wheelhouse. He's taking his shift at the helm, so I knock and open the wheelhouse door. "Can I come in?"

"What's up?" he says, keeping his eyes on the water straight ahead.

"Look, I'm sorry," I say. "I know it was stupid of me. I wanted to check the hull, OK? I guess I just wasn't thinking."

"You don't get it, do you? The Commission doesn't want us out here. You can't just go snooping around. That's asking for trouble. What if they pull the plug on this whole trip? Or worse." Watching his profile snapping at me like that irks me. His blond hair hangs perfectly tussled over his forehead. My cheeks flush as I remember the feeling of his arrogant hands around my waist in the water this morning. Apology is the last thing on my mind now.

"Oh, come on," I say, "I saw something on the anchor line. I wasn't snooping for anything. And anyway, what gave you the right to go grabbing me like that?"

He whips his head around to face me. "What gave you the right to go swimming in the first place, or to pull me into your stunt? The way I see it, I saved your silly butt, and you almost got me in trouble."

"You're pretty full of yourself," I throw back with a little less resolve. I did the wrong thing, but I'm not ready to back down.

He takes a breath, struggling to wipe the anger from his face. "Like it or not," he says forcing that irritatingly friendly first mate voice, "it's part of my job to keep everyone on this boat safe and to keep this expedition on track."

In spite of myself, I'm beginning to see it from his perspective. If the Commission pulls the plug, he and his father will probably have nothing left. The Fouling has shut down everything in the Caribbean and the Gulf of Mexico from diving to fishing, to tourism of any sort. Jake and Sully could end up like the rest of the Fouling's victims. People who have lost everything. They live in their cars or makeshift shanty towns in open fields or public parks.

When it first started, Felicia and I took up a collection at school for the victims. Without fail, the kids whose families ran tourist businesses or lobster boats gave the most. But charity ran dry when the Fouling continued to advance. Worries shifted to what would happen if it crept north into cold water. The experts say it would take years to get here, but that's not what it looks like from the news reports. My whole town relies on the water, not just boating people. Even Felicia's mom who hates the water depends on it. She's an accountant for a barge company that would sink in no time if the Fouling made its way up the coast. My dad would be a wreck trying to keep the marine labs working at the University. The whole department would go under. If there was no work on the water, the town would shut down and the devastation would spread like the plague until it paralyzed the entire East Coast.

"What was it like when the Fouling started?" I blurt out without thinking.

He looks taken aback. "You want to know what it was like? It sucked. That's what it was like!"

This time, I really didn't mean to push his buttons. "I'm sorry," I say. "I shouldn't have asked that."

After a few awkward minutes of silence, I shuffle toward the door.

"It was OK at first," he says softly. "We towed in a few boats that got into trouble. No one knew then how bad it would get. Then we started picking up our own boats out there."

"Other dive boats?" I ask.

"We had four others," he nods, "bigger than this one. They had regular diesel engines. My dad built this one, mostly to see if it could be done—a solar electric boat.

"He had twenty-two crew members to support with that fleet. He didn't want to put them out of work, so I just kept scraping the Fouling off the bottoms, and we kept sending the boats back out. We kept advertising, and divers kept coming."

"That was good of your dad to keep his crew working." I don't know what else to say.

"Yep, well, now it's just me," Jake snaps. "So, what about you? Have you done much diving?"

The subject of the Fouling is closed. "I dive all the time," I tell him, glad for the shift to a more pleasant topic. "I was certified four years ago. Mostly I dive in the cold water up north."

"So, you're a drysuit diver?"

"I'd be a fool to do that in a wetsuit," I say, feeling a little pride welling up. Drysuit diving takes special training because your suit is basically a big air bag. It keeps you dry, and you can wear warm clothes underneath it, but as you go down, the water squeezes the suit around you like a boa constrictor.

"You like that kind of diving?" he asks.

"Yeah, actually. I like the challenge." The whole idea is that you have to balance yourself in the water. On the way down, you shoot a little burst of air into your suit from your tank to relieve the pressure and keep you from sinking like a rock. On the way up, the air inflates and you have to vent it out so you don't shoot to the surface like a runaway balloon. It's not so hard once you get the feel of it, but it takes training and practice to stay in control.

"Sounds like maybe you like a little danger, too," Jake adds, and I hope he's not going to start in on me again about this morning. Drysuit diving is only dangerous if you're not careful, or you don't know what you're doing. For one thing, you have to know to keep your feet below your shoulders, or the air in your suit rushes to your feet and flips you upside-down. If that happens, and you don't know how to roll out of it, you can't vent the suit on the way up. You end up rocketing to the surface feet first and out of control. Anytime you shoot to the surface too fast, it can be deadly.

"That's not true," I argue, "I'm not searching for thrills if that's what you mean."

"Whatever you say," Jake says. "Are you studying to be a marine biologist, or something?"

"Or something." It's all I've ever really wanted to be, but don't feel like going all best friends and telling him about my life.

"Or something, huh? Me too," he says.

"You're in school?"

"Was. I quit in October. Would have graduated high school this year if it weren't for the Fouling. I got in to Harvard and Oxford, but I had to come help keep the boats going." Oxford? Who even applies to Oxford? He must be some seriously hot shot student. I try to imagine Jake hunched over a library table at a university, but it doesn't fit. He looks like he should be hanging out at the beach flashing his perfect white-toothed smile at flirty girls in bikinis. I think I've totally misjudged Jake.

I'm glad I didn't tell him I left school on purpose for this. He's here struggling to keep his father's business going, while I'm getting school credit for this whole trip as long as I keep a journal and write a report about it. I envision him doing all the dirty work, scraping and painting his father's boats as fast as they could haul them out just to get them back in the water. "You can still go back to school, right?"

"We'll see. Everything is kind of up in the air, you know." He's trying to make it sound as if it's no big deal, but he keeps staring forward. The disparity of our circumstances hangs in the air between us.

Then, despite myself, I just blurt out the one thing that's

been on my mind all day. "What do you think it was?" Instantly, I can tell he understands what I'm talking about. His eyes narrow, and for a minute, I think he's going to yell at me to get out.

"I don't know, but it was creepy," he says.

"Do you think it could be a recent wreck? Something sunk by the—"

"I don't know," he cuts me off and looks over his shoulder as if someone might overhear us. It's not smart to accuse the Commission out loud. When they were formed more than 50 years ago, they were supposed to be an international peace keeping alliance—an Ocean Security Commission put together with special military units from 24 countries. Their whole mission was to get rid of the brutal dictator of the Cubbarros, but after they accomplished that, there always seemed to be other threats that needed to be contained. They set up a base on Cubbarros, and the founding countries kept supplying them with money and weapons. The Commission just kept building up their military. They started taking more power over the oceans, even setting up "sanctioned" shipping lanes and charging taxes for anyone traveling on the water. Eventually, they became so powerful, and so secretive, that the founding countries lost control over them. The Commission recruits soldiers and sailors from around the world, now, but no one really knows who's in charge or who's working for them.

Even the most powerful governments don't seem to want to challenge them. The Commission rules the entire Atlantic, and boats that don't play by their rules end up dry docked for good, or at the bottom of the ocean.

It didn't occur to me this morning that going in the water for five minutes to check the bottom of the boat might put me face to face with that reality. I was more worried about the Fouling, but now that I've seen something, I can't pretend I didn't.

Obviously, that's just what Jake wants to do. "Whatever it is," he continues, "it's not our business right now. If anyone knew we were looking around in a blackout zone, I'm thinking it would be pretty hard to explain. As it is, our little cover was pretty thin."

"*Your* little cover made *me* look stupid." I don't want to get into it again, but my cheeks burn at the memory of his face so close to mine, and the idea of what Dirk must think of me. I haven't even known Jake twenty-four hours, and Dirk thinks we were flirting. It probably even looked like we were kissing.

"Stupid?" he says. "How do you think you would have looked if Dirk heard you shouting 'What was that, did you see it?'" Jake wobbles his head back and forth mocking my voice. Then he narrows his eyes at me. "I don't know what it was. Some old shipwreck, some sunken military thing, some nothing. I don't want to know, and neither should you."

That may be true, but I can't believe he isn't the least bit curious. "Well then, fine," I say, standing up to leave. "It's gone anyway. We'll never see it again, so whatever."

His stare follows me to the door. "Alannis, please stay out of trouble," he says, as I reach for the knob.

Outside again, I make my way forward along the side rail to the end of the main cabin. I don't want to go inside where I might have to talk to someone or up on the bow where someone might see me. So, I slide down and lean my back against the cabin. My head sinks into my hands. I just wanted to be on a research trip. I didn't intend to look like an idiot on day one.

We're traveling full speed, and the wind whips my hair

into a tangled mop, but I'm thankful for the fresh air. Until the scent of Guillermo's cigar snakes around the corner along with his voice. He must be standing against the cabin on the foredeck. He's talking quietly, but the sound carries on the rush of air.

"You do not understand, my friend."

"Don't worry about it, Jerry" Dirk says. "It's all good."

"No, it is not." The heaviness in Guillermo's voice sounds dramatic in his wordy sing-song accent. "We were not supposed to be there, and now they have seen."

My breath catches in my throat. I'm frozen. He knows we saw the wreck.

"They won't harm us," Dirk says. "I've got your back, man. I won't let'em anywhere near you." Wait, who are they talking about?

"Maybe it has been a long time since I was a boy, yes?" Guillermo is so close I can hear the crackle of burning tobacco as he sucks on his cigar. There is a long, slow exhale and sickeningly sweet smoke wafts over my head. "But I know them. They will watch us. Such a mistake again and they will kill us all."

The fresh air I came out here to find feels neither fresh nor safe. I lift myself onto trembling knees and crawl backward silently to the door of the main cabin.

CHAPTER 4

INSIDE THE MAIN SALON, THE REST OF THE SCIENCE TEAM IS sitting at the settee, going over papers and looking at something on Candace's laptop. I'm desperate to tell Lacey what I just overheard, but she's boxed into the settee. It's like a restaurant booth with bench seats on three sides, and she's sitting in the middle. I can't think of a good excuse to get her to come to our cabin, so I sit down next to Matt. My heart is racing. Do they know we're being followed?

"Have you been out getting some sun?" Lacey quips.

"I was up at the wheel with Jake." As soon as the words are out a wave of embarrassment hits me. If they know about this morning, maybe they think I was snooping around, jeopardizing our lives. And even worse, maybe they think I was in the water—putting us in danger—to flirt with the first mate. My mouth has gone dry. We should be going back home before the Commission decides they want us out of here.

Sully should be telling Jake to turn around, but he's giving some kind of instruction to Matt. "There's plenty in the supply locker. Help yourself."

"Thanks," Matt answers, "but that kind of sunscreen gives my face a rash. I'll stick with the zinc." He curls his finger into a plastic jar and pulls out a glob of bright white sun block. He smears it on the bridge of his nose.

Lacey has turned back to Candace, "So, what do you

think? Two morning dives, and two in the afternoon?" They don't sound worried about anything. I feel like they should be doing something. Searching the horizon for Commission boats. Getting ready to leave. Something. Their normalcy is disorienting.

Guillermo steps inside wearing a full, hearty smile. He's a short man with a big presence whose joviality fills the room. "So, my friends, have you decided where we will picnic tomorrow?" He pulls the stool out from under the counter that separates the galley from the rest of the salon. It's attached beneath the counter and swivels out to lock in place. It reminds me of the stool my dentist sits in as he hovers over me with sharp, probing instruments. But there is nothing probing about the way Guillermo looks at us now. He doesn't act the least bit worried about being tracked down and killed. Dirk walks in and stands against the wall. He folds his arms over his chest and crosses one ankle over the other. This is his default stance.

He looks calm, and he isn't telling us to turn around and go back. The whole group exudes a sense of anticipation while they plan the first few dives. Except for my unshakable anxiety, it feels, for the first time, the way I imagined it would. Like the beginning of an expedition.

When we arrive on site in the late afternoon, one tiny strip of land marks the break between ocean and sky like a pencil smudge on the western horizon. Jake and Sully plunge into the water to check the bottom of the boat. "Finally," I think to myself. We left the marina yesterday afternoon, and the boat sat in the water all day before leaving. By now, the Fouling could be inches thick.

Sully pops up with a big smile. "Aside from the slightest bit of plain old algae, she's clean as a whistle," he says.

Everyone's shoulders seem to relax in relief, as if we had all been holding back a little bit of breath, just in case.

"What'd you see down there?" Dirk asks.

Sully sounds like a tour guide. "You're going to love it. Big fish all over the place." He doesn't mention if there was Fouling down on the reef, but I'm sure it must be thick.

A few months ago, the last time a group of divers went out into the Caribbean, the Fouling was just starting to spread across the reef in thick patches. It's unlike anything scientists have seen before. The experts say it looks like an organism that supposedly went extinct with the dinosaurs almost 66 million years ago. They don't know where it came from, or why it's suddenly spreading, but that's why we're here. Candace found reports that suggest the Fouling was here hundreds of years ago. She thinks it may have lived here naturally without causing any damage until the oil spill happened. The spill provided an abundance of food that enabled it to spread like wildfire. If the Fouling lived here in balance with the rest of the reef before, we may be able to find something here that eats it, or out-competes it, or somehow kept it under control all those years.

"Be ready for the first dive in an hour," Candace says to the group. "Alannis, you'll be diving with me until you get used to the way we collect data."

That's awesome. I'm going to be diving with Candace. THE Dr. Candace Warren that is, world renown marine biologist. And me, Alannis Summers, her dive partner. This is my chance to really show her what I can do. So far, I don't think I've made a very good impression.

*

This first dive is just a scouting trip. Each team will swim out from the boat to get a visual on how much Fouling is down there. Candace and I are the first ones ready, so we move to the platform to jump in.

Dirk watches my every move. Like a seasoned diver, I hold my gauges close to me so they won't bang against the boat. He cranes his neck to see all the different parts of my gear, as if I might have it on wrong. Determined to ignore him, I adjust my mask and flop my way down the step to the edge of the platform. I move comfortably and with confidence, but there is no way to look graceful out of water in diving gear. Aside from the awkwardness of walking in clown-sized feet, I have to lean forward to balance the weight of the tank on my back. It's strapped to a buoyancy compensator, a BC. It's a bulky vest with wide plastic buckles in front. Add to that a fat belt with chunky weights that help me stay down at the bottom, and even a prima ballerina couldn't make this look graceful, but I'm trying. Hoses stick out of the valve at the top of my tank and reach over my shoulders like tentacles. One attaches to the BC so I can I inflate it or deflate it to keep me perfectly stable at any depth. Another one attaches to the regulator I'm just about to plug into my mouth.

Holding my mask to my face, I step forward into the glassy blue below. It takes just a split second for the plunge, but I love the feeling of anticipation right before hitting the water. When we're both in, Candace and I let some air out of our BCs and sink down into the cool water. The familiar feeling of breathing underwater and the light mechanical sound of the regulator are like instant meditation. I inhale, a soft inward *shhhhh* of breath followed by the deep *whooshhhh* and the gurgle of bubbles out.

I'm suddenly swarmed by more fish than I've ever seen in my life. A school of silver jacks flashes by, and dozens of sergeant majors form a cloud around me—white fish with wide black bars like prison suits. They escort Candace and me to the bottom where an array of colors and textures overwhelm me. Bulbous hard corals and branching sea fans waving in the current. Anemones and sponges. The noise is an outrageous cacophony of snapping and crunching. The sound of a thousand fish nibbling at coral or grunting their warnings to one another. It's hard to focus on one thing. Candace points into the distance to tell me which direction we're heading. Sharks prowl the water column midway between the surface and the reef below with a slow side to side sweep of head and tail. It seems to be just reef sharks. Mostly harmless, but I've never seen so many. Blue grey shadows weaving in and out against a blue background. We swim close to the bottom, examining a kaleidoscope of colors, and searching for any sign of the Fouling. An hour passes like minutes.

When Candace taps me on the shoulder, signaling it's time to return to the boat, I realize I've strayed from the task. Distracted by the abundance of life down here, I've almost forgotten about the black crust I'm supposed to be looking for.

We're the last to surface. The other scientists are chattering like a team that just won a big game. "That was awesome," Lacey cries. "That is the healthiest reef I've ever seen."

"Unbelievable," Dirk says in the most amiable tone I've heard from him so far.

"Magnificence I thought I would never see again," Guillermo adds. We compare our dives, each of us describing the remarkable things we saw.

As we hang our gear to dry, Candace mentions the Fouling. "I didn't see any sign of it," she begins. "If it's here, something is keeping it in check. It's going to be hard to find." After what we saw in the marina, this dive brings a burst of hope. We really might find something to stop it.

With the gear put away, the whole team heads straight for the settee where they pour over copies of the three hundred-year-old document Candace found right after the Fouling started. It was written by a Spanish explorer. From his account, he was somewhere off the coast of Cubbarros when he saw something that looks like the Fouling. Parts of this reef should be covered with it.

Guillermo was only twelve when the Commission evacuated his country, but he remembers what he saw growing up here. He used to spearfish in these waters. The black crusty Fouling, he says, was definitely here.

*

At dinnertime, I volunteer to take my turn in the galley. I pull Lacey over to help me in the cramped little kitchen. I still have a lot of things I want to talk with someone about. I start by asking her how she knows Dirk is an agent.

"Doesn't he just look like one?" Lacey asks. "I'll put money on it. He has that straight up, no-nonsense posture. As if he's observing everything with those dark eyes." Lacey seems more excited than nervous about the idea of a Commission agent on board with us.

"Do you think he could keep us safe?" I ask her. "I mean, if the Commission were following us or something." She just laughs as if it was a dumb question.

She leans into me gently, chiding me, "Jake's kind of cute, huh?" Seriously? Is this important? If she is referring to our swim, Dirk has been talking. I would like to tell her right now what really happened this morning, and why Dirk saw what he thinks he saw between me and Jake. I want her to know about the shipwreck, and what I heard Guillermo and Dirk say. But I can't get her off the subject of Jake.

"I find him annoying," I say. "Especially the way he

explains everything to us like we've never been on a boat before."

"It's his job, remember. He's a dive jockey," Lacey says. "He's used to taking tourists out diving." Although she's arguing in his defense, it sounds more condescending than she realizes. There's nothing wrong with being a "dive jockey," but I know he'd rather be here doing science like the rest of us. For some reason, I want her to know that, and I feel a twinge of defensiveness for him that irritates me more than he does. I didn't ask for his sob story, and I don't want to feel guilty for being a part of the research team while he plays the part of the hired crew.

"Lacey, I'm absolutely not interested in Jake. He's totally not my type." She's not ready to let me off the hook.

"I know you guys were swimming this morning. It's no big deal. Why are you so worried about it? Do you have a boyfriend or something?"

"No," I snap reflexively. Her nosiness irritates me. Why is it always about boyfriends? I don't have a boyfriend because guys who are friends are so much easier to get along with. I've had some totally datable guy friends, but whenever I've gone out with any of them it's ruined everything. They suddenly go all possessive and controlling. "It's not what you think, with Jake," I tell Lacey. "Besides, it was stupid, I shouldn't have gone in the water at all."

"Well, that's probably true. But I don't think anyone was too worried about it." Lacey didn't see the look on Dirk's face, but she seems right about one thing: no one else is acting concerned. Even Dirk and Guillermo look at ease sitting around the table with Candace and Matt.

She elbows me again. "I think everyone understands. A dive boat can be a very romantic place." Everyone? So everyone knows? This is not the way I had planned to start the trip. As it is, I already feel I have to convince Candace I belong here.

When I met Dr. Warren the first time, I made such a poor impression that I almost can't believe I'm sitting here. It was last fall, shortly after she moved to New England. My dad had just hired her to become the head of the Department of Marine Biology and Ecology. He invited her to dinner. I had a vision of stimulating conversation about important research topics. I had planned to demonstrate my superior understanding of marine ecology. But the minute she walked in the door, that vision vaporized. Underneath her warm smile was something disciplined and unyielding. Something that made it clear she was not easily impressed. That she did not tolerate fools. I have never been so conscious of my tendency to flail my hands and ramble right into other people's words. I sat through the dinner conversation mutely, careful not to screech my knife across the plate. She terrified me.

Three weeks ago, I met her for the second time, and I was determined to redeem myself. My Dad had been all excited to tell us about this expedition over dinner. He was sure Dr. Warren was right about the Fouling. When he mentioned that she needed assistants because she was still new at the university, he had no idea I would see that as a chance of a lifetime.

The next day, I showed up at her office without calling and offered my help on the trip. I was pretty sure she would refuse at first, but I also knew she had less than a month to assemble a team.

I didn't know Lacey then, but I knew Dr. Warren had a new research assistant from California who would be going, for sure. Everyone else who worked for Dr. Warren before she moved to New England had found other jobs. Only her former lead assistant was willing to leave his new position to come on this expedition. That was Matt.

Dr. Warren would have eventually found someone else, but there I was, eager, persistent, and—as far as I'm concerned—qualified. With no emotion, she stared at me from across her desk. My carefully typed three page resume listing all my accomplishments lay untouched beneath her crossed hands.

It occurred to me then, if she kicked me out and word got back to my father that I had barged into one of his professor's offices behind his back, I would be in deep trouble. As per plan, I tried to stay calm and professional, making it clear I wasn't going to take "no" for an answer. My heartbeat throbbed in my ears, and it felt like I was waiting forever for her to say something. Then she leaned forward, interlaced her fingers, and said, "Fine." I sat there staring blankly for a minute, expecting her to smile or welcome me to the team. Anything. None of that happened. So, I rose from my seat clumsily, saying, "Great. Thanks. Well, that's great," and made a dash for the door.

Before I got there, she said in a flat voice, "I'll let the dive officer know you'll be getting in touch with him for your check out dives." She was already sliding my unread resume off to one side of her desk.

*

Our morning dives are just like the first. We're in 30 feet of water, and we see nothing but amazing and beautiful reef. There is no sign of the Fouling. After lunch, Candace and I scour an outcropping of coral, hoping to find even the smallest sign of it. It's so dense with life. I could hover here forever and still not see everything. A field of two-inch tall Christmas tree worms stands like a miniature forest of feathery, snow tipped evergreens from a Dr. Seuss story. I poke my finger toward one of them, and they all disappear back into their tiny tubes. The slug-like nudibranch crawling over a patch of brain coral looks like a piece of candy with its bright yellow skin and blue ringed spots.

We have been down for more than an hour. The others have already come to the surface, and Candace signals it's time for us to leave. We begin our brief ascent together, but I'm so enthralled by the scenery that I hang back, floating a few feet below the surface. I'm waiting for her to get out first. A small fish swims right up to my mask, and I try to touch it. It's iridescent green with black stripes and it moves fluidly around my hand as I wave my fingers back and forth in the water. It's as if we're dancing, this little fish and I. Dr. Warren removes her weight belt and hoists it on the platform before kicking herself out of the water. The heavy belt clatters as it lands and the sound scares my little fish. He zips back down toward a coral outcropping and takes refuge behind a patch of something black and filamentous. It's waving like hair. I can't put my finger on it, but something about it seems out of place. I squint to get a better look.

It is hair. And a forehead. Beneath that. . . two black eyes stare right at me.

CHAPTER 5

WITHOUT WAITING FOR DR. WARREN TO GET OUT OF THE water, I break for the surface and flail to the other side of the platform. My mask is gone. My regulator has fallen out of my mouth. I'm coughing up water.

Dirk grabs the valve at the top of my dive tank and pulls me clear out of the water onto the platform. He grabs my chin with one hand and tells me to look at him. "You OK? Are you all right?"

"I'm OK." I cough. "I'm fine. . ."

He grabs the hose that has my dive computer on it. There are no flashing lights on the small black console. No warnings. "Did you bolt?" he asks, meaning, did I bolt to the surface from the bottom.

"No, I'm good, I'm fine." If I had bolted, my lungs could have burst like an over-filled balloon and caused an embolism. Something like that could kill me right here, right now. I'm still choking and trying to figure out what I saw. It happened so fast. "My mask—" I turn to look back into the water. I must have ripped it off before I even hit the surface.

Jake knows something is not right. He stands on deck above the dive platform, looking at me with his chin tucked in and his brows lifted in question. He just barely shakes his head to the side. A small "no". He rolls his eyes as if I've just frustrated him. *Don't go looking for trouble,* his expression warns, *and don't freak out in front of everyone.*

When I get back on deck, Sully grabs a mask and jumps in. "I'll get your mask," he calls.

"I'm right behind you," Dirk yells back, but Sully is already gone.

I'm still coughing up water. "Are you OK?" Candace asks me in a flat voice. Her cool, disapproving look reminds me of the first time we met.

By the time Dirk gets his mask and fins on, Sully has already been down a few minutes. Candace and I have taken off our tanks and are peering over the edge to look for him. He's been down there for a long time with whatever it is.

Sully finally pops up with my mask in his hand. "You're like a fish," Matt says. "You were down so long, I was beginning to think you had gills." Sully blows it off, but Jake jumps into the conversation.

"Ex-Navy SEAL. Don't worry, once he gets going, you'll hear the stories." There is more than a little sarcasm in Jake's tone. Sully shoots him a look over his shoulder.

"No stories to tell," he says flatly. I'm still shaking.

Once everyone is back on deck, and I have stopped coughing, they look at me expectantly, waiting for an explanation. I can't tell them I saw a person watching me down there. So, I stutter the first thing that comes to my mind. "I thought I saw a shark." Immediately I regret it. We have seen sharks all day long. Mostly black tipped reef sharks and lemon sharks. Some of them are ten feet long, but they're harmless. A part of any tropical reef dive. It's no reason to flip out. I'm disappointed that they seem to believe me.

While the excitement calms down, and we return to our routine of putting away gear, I grow increasingly embarrassed. Candace has no tolerance for incompetence, and I'm beginning to look incompetent. By dinner time, I've regained my composure. I've been running through the possibilities. What could I have seen that looked like a pair of eyes? Nothing clicks, but there has to be an explanation for what I saw.

Candace and Dirk toss around ideas about why there is no Fouling here. They agree that the reef is so healthy, it would probably be resilient to the Fouling. Most reefs and shorelines are in such bad shape from overfishing, development and pollution that, when a new species like the Fouling finds its way there, it invades without any competition. Here, there is such diversity that no one organism has an advantage over the others.

"I've dived in every ocean in the world," Dirk says, "and I've never seen some of these things before."

"No kidding," Matt adds. "Those Goliath grouper must have been a couple hundred pounds." We're all excited by the size of the fish. Goliath grouper are endangered in many places, and big ones like that haven't been seen in decades. Some of the fish we've seen were even thought to be extinct. They were everywhere, and they were huge.

Matt insists he saw a grouper the size of a small car. "He could have swallowed me whole," he says dryly. "I'm not kidding." There is the slightest hint of excitement in his voice. I think he's telling the truth.

"It's wild the way they swim right up to you and hang there, watching," Lacey says. "And there was something big that kept swimming up behind me and darting away."

Sully looks up from his plate with a mouth half full of food. "What do you think it was," he asks. I look at him for signs of recognition. Did he see those eyes when he went in to get my mask?

"I never got a good look at it," Lacey answers. "It moved

41

too quickly." Sully's attention returns to his dinner. He didn't see anything. "I know there are no sea lions here, but that's what it felt like," Lacey continues. "I've dived around them in the kelp forests in California. Sometimes they hang around just out of sight, and then dart by when you're not looking."

Dirk straightens his shoulders and leans back against his seat. "You're right about that, Lace." He's gotten into the habit of nicknaming everyone. Guillermo is now Jerry. I'm Al, and Jake is just "J." He tried calling Candace "Candy" once, but she shut that down with one look. "There are no sea lions out here, but we've got dolphins," he says. "You know where I'm going with this, don't you, Sully?"

Sully keeps chewing.

"I've had the honor of doing some training with navy divers," Dirk continues. He talks through the rest of dinner about how the navy trains sea lions and dolphins to perform underwater missions. He says they can attach bombs to things, and carry messages and cameras. Sometimes they sneak into enemy territory and take surveillance pictures. "They're smart weapons," he says. "Kind of like animal spies. So human-like."

"Human-like?" I say, trying to form a clear picture in my mind of what I saw.

"You got it," he says. "Did you see it, too?"

Could we be talking about the same thing? "It had black hair and two eyes peering over the coral at me." As I'm saying it, I realize how ridiculous it sounds.

Matt's eyes widen, and he begins whistling an eerie tune. "Oooh, dolphin-man, we're definitely in the Triad now." I've got to backpedal quickly, so I attempt to chuckle with bravado as if I was just joking. I hope it doesn't sound like I was making fun of Dirk.

Either way, humor is lost on Candace. She spreads her

hands on the edge of the table as if smoothing out a tablecloth that isn't there. "Whether you're seeing some kind of elusive dolphin, or curious fish, I have no doubt there are many surprises on this reef," she says, "but let's not get ourselves all worked up."

Matt moves his hand like a shark swimming in the water. "Maybe it was a shark-man," he says, throwing the joke back on me. Everyone laughs except Candace. I try to laugh convincingly along with them. I wish I thought it was funny.

Dinner conversation dwindles, and Guillermo and Candace stay on the upper deck while the rest of us clear the table and go about our jobs. One of mine is to help Dirk set up the dive gear for tomorrow.

We're moving to a new dive location in the morning. Guillermo thinks we should get closer to the Islands. It's a little risky because we'll be right up against the blackout zone. Guillermo says if he can see the outlines of land, he can identify his old fishing grounds and lead us to some areas where he remembers the Fouling.

He hasn't seen these islands since he was twelve, when Cubbarros was an independent country. It must have been a whole different life for him then. I've wanted to ask him about his childhood and his culture before the evacuation, maybe include some of his story in my report for school. But however I try to phrase it, I worry it will sound insensitive. How do you ask a highly educated, internationally respected scientist what it was like to grow up in a hut and hunt with a spear he made from a stick? How do you ask anyone you don't know well to talk about being ripped from their home? About having their culture erased? Especially when they come from a place with a history like Cubbarros.

Guillermo, like all Cubbarrans, grew up in complete isolation from the rest of the world. For centuries, a long line of dictators had defended the islands from colonization and then refused to trade with other nations. When Navy spies found out what was going on, it shocked the entire world.

The Cubbarran dictator, Barru Pi, had been breeding toxic fish and algae. She had developed powerful poisons from these natural resources, and the Navy said she had been conducting outrageous experiments with them, poisoning some of her own people. There are even rumors that she was using her toxins to breed bizarre, hideous mutants. People said she was responsible for the missing ships in the Triad.

The history books aren't too clear on how she had captured ships, or how the rulers before her had fought off so many attempts to make contact, but apparently, she was very effective at low-tech guerilla warfare—like bandits or pirates or something. She couldn't make modern tools, but she stole what she could from the ships she captured or sunk. Barru Pi adapted whatever she found. People were afraid that if she figured out how to use the technology, she might learn to deliver her poisons around the world. If she understood what she had, she might have even been able to release the nuclear weapons from some of the ships she captured. There was also a good chance she would blow up her whole country by accident.

People were so shaken by what could have happened that the Ocean Security Commission was formed practically overnight. They swarmed the Cubbarros islands to rescue the people from Barru Pi's dictatorship. The idea was to bring them democracy and help them become part of the modern world.

Of course, it didn't work out that way. When the

Commission got there, they found out most of the land and surrounding waters were toxic, poisoned by Barru Pi's experiments. They evacuated everyone on the islands. Guillermo and his family became instant refugees and were scattered around the world. He hasn't even been allowed to visit his homeland once.

The Commission set up their base on Cubbarros so they could clean up the environment. The islands were kept off limits partly because they were toxic, but also because no one wanted Barru Pi's weapons to get into the wrong hands. Some people say the Commission didn't destroy all of them because they're conducting experiments of their own. Whether that's true or not, no one but Commission officers has set foot on Cubbarros since.

Right after they took over the Cubbarros, the Commission started patrolling the Atlantic, monitoring small island nations to keep dictators from gaining power. Eventually, the Commission started protecting cargo ships from hijackers—modern-day pirates, they said. That's where our history books stop talking about the Commission. That's when I think the power started shifting and people started to fear them. I'm sure that's when Cubbarrans lost all hope of returning to their islands.

Guillermo looks tense, but he says we need to move closer so he can see landmarks that will help him find the Fouling. I can't tell if he really wants to get closer or not. Is he excited to see the island, or does it bring back such horrible memories of life under Barru Pi that he doesn't want to be here at all? Either way, when we move to our new dive site, we're going to have to be very careful not to wander back into the blackout zone. The vision of that sunken ship sticks with me.

I'm moving empty tanks to the compressor for filling when Dirk comes back and starts the engine. The compressor is the only piece of equipment on the boat that runs on gas, and it's loud. Just as he said he would, Dirk double-checks all the dive computers against the dive plans he and Candace wrote. The dive computers are consoles the size of a TV remote. They tell us how much air is in our tanks and keep track of how long we dive and how deep we go. For a dive safety officer, or perhaps even an agent of the Commission, they reveal exactly what we've been doing down there.

As I'm checking the air pressure in each tank, he asks me, "Do you like diving?"

Obviously I do, or I wouldn't be here. "Sure. I love it."

"What did you list on your dive chart? Something like 400 dives?" He has no business looking at my records. "You must have been diving in diapers."

"I was 12 when I started," I try to sound casual, and prepare to defend myself for this morning.

"I guess that would make you pretty comfortable in the water, usually." His voice is matter-of-fact, which makes it feel even more intrusive. "I've been diving up in New England," he says. "Not a lot of visibility. Lots of dark shadows. Seen lots of shark on my dives up there."

I'm quiet. Up north we see sand sharks on nearly every dive. They're big and menacing with jagged gnarly teeth sticking out in all directions. Someone with as many dives as I have doesn't flinch at sharks. Unless maybe it's a mako or great white. Even then, the last thing you want to do is thrash around like I did today.

"You ever bolted to the surface back home?" he probes.

His tone is accusatory. Is he suggesting I lied about my dive experience? I'm not about to take that accusation without a fight. "I didn't bolt," I say. "I was practically at the surface. I've never freaked out before, and I wasn't actually freaked out anyway."

"You've got a lot of fire for a kid," he says, which irks the heck out of me. "I bet you're not easily intimidated."

I don't know if he thinks I'm lying about my dive record or about what I saw underwater, but he's fishing for something. The idea that he may actually be some kind of agent is unnerving. Telling him I saw a face watching me and a shipwreck I shouldn't have seen doesn't seem like much of an option. I hate to do it, but I go for the nervous diver excuse. "I'm just a little creeped out with so many sharks around." I put on what feels like a sickeningly sappy face. "All those big fish darting so close behind our backs. It's just scary, that's all."

Whether he buys it or not, Lacey interrupts us on the back deck with a bag of Oreos in her hand. "There you guys are; anybody want some?" She offers the bag to me and then to Dirk. Even though Oreos are my favorite, I say no. It's the perfect opportunity to leave. Lacey has been trying to find out more about Dirk since we left Florida. Now it's his turn to sit under her microscope. Go to it, Lacey!

Matt's in the galley cutting himself a slice of chocolate cake which he offers to hand over to me. I devour it right there next to him before he has even finished cutting another slice for himself. At the settee, Jake leafs through a fish identification book while Sully sits next to him winding his dive watch.

Matt taps me on the shoulder. "Want me to show you how to set up the scopes?" he mumbles through a mouthful of cake.

Beyond filling tanks, I haven't been of much use to the team yet, so I'm thankful for the opportunity to learn something. We go below to the cabin across from mine. This is where Matt has been spending so much time, and now I understand why. He has unpacked all the boxes of gear we brought with us. He's organized a temporary laboratory, and posted labels all over the place to identify where things go. He shows me how the equipment is arranged and where the data gets logged, and explains how to handle the microscopes. They have to be set up and broken down every day, because a rocking boat is no place for sensitive equipment.

Matt is in his element, the master of this little world he's created. After running me through the procedure, he has me do it a few times myself for practice. Battening down the notebooks, stacking the slides and petri dishes, securing the scopes in their cases, re-adjusting the bungies and straps beneath the microscope platforms. He's surprisingly patient with me when I misread the labels, and when I leave one of the instruments unsecured. Twice.

We'd better have more luck finding Fouling tomorrow or we won't have a use for any of this equipment. By my third time setting up, I'm trying to stay focused, but I keep fumbling as if I have two left hands. All I can think about is our last dive, and those eyes.

The vision of them keeps me awake most of the night.

CHAPTER 6

THE NEXT MORNING, I'M GROGGY AND TIRED, AND WHEN we drop anchor, I'm not looking forward to getting back in the water. The high peaks of one of the Cubbarros Islands have grown from a smudge to a series of bumps on the horizon. It's as close as we can get, but Guillermo says it's enough for him to navigate by.

When Candace and I dive to the bottom, I scan around in all directions. Sleek steel-blue sharks and schools of silvery jacks fill the water column far in the distance. I look down at the reef. My eyes jump from one dark patch to the next. They're open so wide, it kind of hurts. Everything looks suspect. The long arms of a tube-dwelling anemone float upward like white hair. Fingers of black corkscrew anemone reach out from beneath a crevice. A speeding school of four-eyed butterfly fish spills over the reef in front of me like a waterfall. With one real eye at the front, and a false eye spot in the back near their tail, they seem to be mocking me. Swimming like a fast moving stream around me, over me, and back down behind a coral outcropping.

Then I feel what Lacey was talking about. Something in the water behind me. I whip around and catch a flash zipping off into the distance. Thick clouds of fish swim past us in rapid bursts, but I see nothing that wasn't there before. Again, and again, I feel that presence behind me. Once or twice, Candace glances over her shoulder, and I follow her eyes. Still nothing. It's exhausting, this state of high alert. Checking behind me constantly. Studying everything that waves or moves in front of me, beside me. Throughout the dive, I see no eyes.

At lunchtime, we eat on the upper deck where Sully has hung a canopy to shade us from the glaring sun. Matt says he felt like he was being watched today, and Dirk launches into another of his stories. They have become predictable.

"One time, in Belize, we were diving at about 150 feet near a sheer drop-off," he says loudly, puffing up his chest yet again. "Nothing but black below. I felt the hairs sitting up on the back of my neck. I looked up and almost swallowed my regulator." An impossibility of course, but he's clearly told this story before. It's picked up a few decorative features along the way. "Right behind me was the open mouth of a whale shark. He looked like a house plowing right toward me." I don't know of any whale sharks the size of a house, but maybe a school bus. Still, everyone here knows they're filter feeders, so they eat plankton, not fish. Definitely not people. They're impressive, but harmless in the end. His ego is driving me crazy.

"What did you do?" Lacey asks. She eggs him on every time.

"I ducked." It's our cue to laugh. "I slipped down over the edge of the drop-off and watched him swim right over me. I even reached up and touched his underside. He was that close."

I guess he's a good scientist or something, because Candace is patient with Dirk's tales. But only to a point. She turns toward Guillermo and says, "It's almost as if those elusive fish are luminescent. I'm certain I've seen a flash or two. They're large, whatever they are. Are you familiar with such a fish?"

Guillermo pauses to relight his cigar. After a few puffs, he has everyone's attention. "Maybe you see sometimes these large fish," he says in his lyrical accent. "Like shadows over your shoulder. They are perrorap. They have many arms, like squid. Men have been snatched from their ships and carried away by the perrorap."

The table is uncomfortably silent. "Have you seen them?" Candace asks.

"It is not good to look at them," he says. "If they choose to, they will hypnotize you with their graceful dance of lights, and then draw you down into the deep."

Lacey pipes in, "They sound like the sirens of the sea who lure sailors with their songs."

Matt disagrees. "Sirens were birds. A squid that jumps from the water and pulls men to their death? Sounds more like the kraken to me." His eyebrows dance on his big round forehead. They pause in mid-leap when he gets to the word "kraken."

"Right?" Lacey joins in, "it's like that pirate movie where the giant squid attacks the ship and takes the whole thing down."

The normally easy-going Cubbarran looks at us with a rigid face. "Do not laugh at what you do not understand. There are many dangers in these waters. Long ago, they listened to Barru Pi. She kept us safe from them. Intruders, she did not protect." An uneasy laugh makes its way around the table. Guillermo points at each of us with his cigar wedged in the crook of two fingers. "You think the Triad is a story of superstition. The sea monsters all myths. Well, my friends, we are the intruders now. And Barru Pi is no longer here to intercede on our behalf."

Sully is the first to break the silence that follows Guillermo's scolding. "Let's agree there's a boat load of crazy stuff down there. Real or myth, doesn't matter. Anyone see something that doesn't look right, you just speak up, huh?" With that, he heads up to the wheelhouse.

The conversation must have shaken Guillermo, because he decides to opt out of the afternoon dives. I would stay behind too, if I could come up with a good excuse. I'm not excited to get back in the water with whatever is down there. Jake is, however. He jumps in to take Guillermo's place as Matt's dive buddy. So far, he and Sully have gone diving once a day to inspect the bottom and do a little sightseeing of their own. But when the science team is in the water, they stay behind to watch and tend us.

It's funny to see Matt and Jake prepping their gear side by side. Matt is tall and square like a loaf of bread stood on end. He leans his shoulders from side to side as he walks to the bench and lays his regulator and BC down in a heap. Jake is tall like Matt, but there's nothing doughy or lumbering about him. He's tan and strong with wide shoulders and a sleek six pack. He looks more confident, more solid, than Matt, even though Matt's easily ten years older. I've watched Jake do this before. Every time he sets up his gear it's like an exact rerun of the last. He holds his BC in his left hand, his regulator in his right, and aligns them carefully next to one another by his tank. His procedure is precise and unwavering. It's obvious he's done this a thousand times. Each time the exact same way.

Sully steps out of the wheelhouse to watch and assist us just as the first diver goes into the water. I dawdle with my gear, hoping Candace isn't in a rush. Eventually, we have to go in. After Guillermo's stories, I'm even more alert than before, but still I see nothing watching me. Maybe Jake has the spirit of Barru Pi in him or something because all afternoon, the strange presence is gone. Even the swarms of sharks have thinned.

*

Over the next couple of days, the secretive fish, or squid, or perrorap, whatever they are, stay away. No eyes watch me from the shadows. Guillermo has returned to his old self. I'm beginning to think it was an illusion.

We still aren't seeing any signs of the Fouling, but new species turn up on every dive. We're collecting samples of sponges and soft corals, slimy algae, and other things the scientists haven't seen before. After Candace saw the notes I was keeping, she realized I actually have some skills and entrusted me with logging in written descriptions of whatever we find on our dives. Apparently she never opened my resume. If she had, she would have known this is what I do best.

I've been a marine science geek my whole life. I used to want to be like that guy who travels around the world making documentaries about all these beautiful underwater places. The scenery was amazing, and I thought it was so cool that you needed all this gear and breathing equipment. It was like exploring another world. He used to open every show with the sentence, "We know more about the surface of Mars than we know about the world beneath our seas." When I learned about the oceans being threatened by global warming, and pollution, and over fishing, I started getting into the whole ecology side of everything, and I was hooked. I went to ocean ecology camps every summer until I was old enough to be a counselor. For the last two years, I've been running a citizen survey program that I started myself in Braverton Bay. Once a month, a group of us survey a few key underwater sites to record information on the ecosystem and post the data on

ScienceNet. It's actually a big deal. The site's a major resource for scientists, and they don't just take anyone's data. They have strict standards.

When Candace asked me to keep the logs, I tried to slip all that information into the conversation. She didn't say anything, but she squeezed her lips together and raised her eyebrows at me. It wasn't much, but I managed to impress her just a little. I'm finally starting to prove my worth on this trip, and the team is settling into a routine, which eases my tension. The scientists spend a lot of time comparing notes on their dives and discussing various research projects they're working on back home. When he's not in the lab, Matt tries to wrangle up a free body to beat at cards or backgammon. I swear I'm going to win before this trip is over.

Lacey studies copies of the old explorer documents. She's translating them from their original Spanish because apparently, she understands it. Her education catches me off guard sometimes. I'm ashamed that I underestimate her because she's bouncy and blond. At some point during each day she makes her way to the bow in one of her string bikinis to work on her lobster tan. Dirk and his enormous ego follow her up there every time. I can't stand his stories, and I avoid him whenever I can. But Lacey tolerates him, somehow. She's not a very quiet person, so I think maybe she just really needs the company.

Sully spends a lot of time in the wheelhouse. Sitting up there with those scrambled eggs on his forehead, I imagine him captaining an aircraft carrier or a battleship. He and Jake dive in the mornings so they can enjoy the scenery before the rest of us go in.

Guillermo has cut back his cigars since Dirk said he would never certify a smoker for diving. Guillermo rolled the cigar between his middle finger and thumb and said, "Well, then, for me it is lucky you do not authorize the diving, no?" He made his point, but now, he only lights up at night, after dinner. He stands at the rail with his soggy stogy, looking out toward his islands. He must wonder if there is anything left of his home. I can't imagine what it was like for him when the Commission came. Guillermo was just a boy, when he was taken away from his islands, from everything he ever knew. In a way, he has already lived through the trauma that victims of the Fouling are experiencing now.

When he is out there, I sneak around to the bow to be alone and listen to the whales. They join us every evening. We can't see them, but their songs fill the night air. Sometimes, the wind carries the faint echo of howler monkeys from the island. Their calls mingle with the soulful cries of the whales. To me, they sound almost magical, and I could stay here forever. Guillermo says they are the sounds of the sea mourning Barru Pi. They make Lacey uncomfortable, and she says they're giving the team a bad feeling. Whether it's the melancholy songs of the whales or the fact that we still haven't found any signs of the Fouling, there is definitely a pall hanging over the team.

It's as if we have stepped into another world, as if whatever we left at home was a dream. Or perhaps this is the dream. The nightmare is back home.

CHAPTER 7

IT'S HARD TO BELIEVE WE LEFT FLORIDA ALMOST TWO weeks ago. Our supplies of fresh water and food are running low, so we need to head to shore. The way the expedition was set up, we're expected to check in at the Commission base on Cubbarros to resupply. Sully called on the sat phone last night, and they've downloaded charts for the narrow channel through the reef where we can enter.

The sun has just cleared the horizon when Jake hauls up the anchor. It casts a blinding glare across the flat, calm ocean. I join Sully in the wheelhouse to watch as we get underway.

"Come on up," he says when I peek my head in. Sully can be gruff at times, like when he said there were no stories to tell about his Navy SEAL days, or when he gives Jake orders about running the boat. But when you get him talking about his boat, he's like a proud father showing off. "Come on over here and take the wheel," he says once we're underway. It's a big boat, but it's remarkably stable, and though we're throttled way up, she holds her course. I don't even need to keep my hands on the wheel.

Sully beams at me. "Look at you, young lady, a natural little miss captain." That comment would normally send me through the roof, but I understand he doesn't mean to sound patronizing. He's an old-fashioned navy man who clings to an old order where girls don't become boat captains. I'm not going to change his attitudes. In some odd way, it gives me a chance to relax. I've been so conscious of being the youngest one on this trip. Between my naïve swim in restricted waters and losing control on our first day of diving, I've been working hard to overcome a bad first impression. I haven't been able to be myself. Around Sully, trying to come across as anything other than a girl in high school would be a waste of effort. I sit back and smile easily for maybe the first time in a week.

Jake walks in behind me, ready to take his shift at the helm. Sully backs away from the bridge. "Okey dokey, Jakey, you're up." Before he walks out of the wheelhouse, Sully puts his hands on my shoulders and says, "You need anything, skipper, our first mate here will help you out."

"I think he's taken a liking to you," Jake says as I fix my grip on the wheel.

"Well, he's a nice guy," I reply.

"That's what people say."

"Oh come on, he is nice. You just can't see it because he's your father. You butt heads."

"He's a great guy as long as you don't cross him or get in his way," Jake says. I can imagine that's true. "He's gotten even worse lately. Since everything happened."

He means since the Fouling ruined his business, I'm sure.

"He likes you," Jake says. "I think you remind him of my sister." Nobody has said much about family on this trip, but it surprises me to hear Jake has a sister. With his silky gold highlights and my dark curly frizz, I can't see where the family resemblance would come from. "She's fiery like you," Jake says as if he could read my mind.

"Older or younger?" I ask.

"Older than you," Jake answers flatly. "My twin. How about you, any brothers or sisters?"

I tell him about Alex. He's fourteen. Total opposite of me. Crummy student. His grades aren't very good because he's more interested in cutting up with his friends. He's the one that can make anyone laugh. People love him. Even I can't really be mad at him when he gets me laughing. He's a total rule-follower, though, which means I have plenty of reasons to get mad at him.

He's the one who told my parents about the trip before I had my plan of attack ready. He heard me telling some of my friends about it. Decided my parents should know I had asked one of Dad's professors to "take me on a trip" as he put it. He told them I was planning to "drop out of school" to do it. That didn't go over well. Once I explained how it happened— stretching the truth only slightly about how Dr. Warren seemed really into it, and that I had a plan for keeping up with my schoolwork (that I made up on the spot)—my dad was furious at first. They both reluctantly came around when I compared it to the study abroad program. Some kids spend the end of their junior year in Paris learning how to party in French. I would be living on a boat with a group of adults doing science. I think my dad was even a little bit proud of me for showing so much initiative. My mom decided it would be a great opportunity, and once she accepted the idea, she got into the whole adventure of it.

I don't tell Jake about that. Instead, I tell him about the time I was ten and got stuck in the top of Mr. Clark's tree. Two days before, I had made it halfway up before I fell out and broke my wrist. Even with the cast, I knew I could make it to the top if I took a different route. I just didn't realize I wouldn't be able to make it down. Alex could have talked me down if he wanted to. Telling me which branches to slide down to, which steps to take. Instead, he ran home to tell on me.

Jake doesn't offer any funny stories about his sister. He points to the dolphins that just joined us. One leaps so high out of the water and turns its body sideways before landing. Even from here, I can see it was looking at us. Funny how they show up on our way into the Commission base. As if they're escorting us. I slide off the captain's chair and hand the helm to Jake.

"The last rescue we got was a call from *Iska*," he says, staring straight out at the dolphin. It takes me a minute to realize he's talking about rescuing ships stranded because of the Fouling. "She was ours. Fourty miles from Bermuda," he continues, "but we were four days away, towing a fishing boat with six men on board. We tried to call for someone else to help *Iska*, but by then, most boats were out of the water. No one was willing to risk going back in."

The dolphins are everywhere, leaping and spinning. They look like they're having so much fun. I'm wondering if this is one of those amazing stories of animals rescuing humans. *Dolphin Saves Boat and All Her Crew.*

"The Fouling had gotten inside the engine water intake, and it was locking up," Jake continues. "We were in a real bad position. *Iska*, a crew of five, and eighteen passengers drifting 40 miles from shore. And us still days away, dragging that fishing boat behind us. The Fouling was bringing the fishing boat down in the stern, and I'll swear she was growing heavier by the hour.

"My dad decided we had to cut it loose," Jake continues. I'm still waiting for the happy part, but I can't hear it coming in his voice. "The fishing boat captain was angry, but it was starting to look like she was going to sink anyway, maybe drag us all down with her. Once we let her go, we headed straight for *Iska*. We had the whole fishing crew on this boat, and I didn't know how we were going to get everyone from *Iska* on board, but there wasn't time to go back to shore."

Jake bends his head down. He wipes his hand across his forehead and over his face. His jaw tenses underneath the blond stubble. "There was a storm. It was getting rough. We were still maybe a day out. We ran at night off battery for as long as we could. Joe, *Iska*'s captain, kept calling in. When *Iska* started listing to port, she took on water pretty quickly."

"Julie was the last person. . . " Jake trails off. The sun glare off the water hurts my eyes. I want to ask who Julie is. Instead, I shift around in my seat through the silence.

"Did you reach them?" I ask.

After a few minutes that seem like hours he begins again. "We could hear the wind howling over the radio. Joe had to yell over it, but he sounded calm enough. We told ourselves it wasn't that bad. We'd get there in time. Then he put Julie on."

His voice is stiff and soft, as if he is talking to himself. It feels private, as if my very presence is intrusive. On the other hand, excusing myself would be rude. I stay. I listen.

"Dad and I tried to tell her it was going to be OK. We were going to get there. But her voice. . . My sister never cried. I never, ever saw her cry. She was crying then, telling us the boat was going down fast. Some of the passengers were already in the inflatable life boats. We told her to get her wetsuit on so she would stay warm if they were tossed around in the storm. I don't know what happened. . . We never found anyone."

I turn my head away for his privacy as much as mine. "I'm so sorry, Jake. I can't imagine what that's like."

"We had to tell my mom." I wish he would stop. I don't want to hear more. Thankfully he doesn't seem to want to tell anymore. There isn't anything else to say, so we sit in the wheelhouse watching the dolphins. They have dwindled to just a few now. Below us, Lacey comes to the front of the bow and spreads her beach towel on deck. While she rubs oil on her arms, I realize how incongruous the scene is. As if we are out on vacation.

Dirk joins her and takes up his stance at the rail. Arms crossed over his chest. Legs crossed at the ankles.

*

We pull into the base in Cubbarros in twilight. The dark figures of soldiers line the pier. Their round, helmet-covered heads stand tall. The straight edge of their rifles project from their shoulders. No one waves.

As we get closer, the silence grows more oppressive. The men on the pier don't move, they don't smile. They watch. There's Fouling crusted around the pilings and against the seawall, but it's thin. Nothing like the massive crusty tumors that engulfed Florida. Seeing it for the first time in many days is a stark reminder of the importance of our trip, and a source of frustration at how we're failing so far.

We're not allowed to leave the boat tonight. Our resupply will have to wait until morning. So, Lacey and I eat the last of the Oreos and take turns trying to beat Matt at backgammon. After a half-dozen games, I'm done. It's hopeless. I head to my bunk.

In the morning, the sky is overcast, and a steady rain falls, bouncing off the surface of the water. Only two people are allowed ashore. Guillermo and Matt walk down the pier with our wish-list in their pockets. I would have expected it to be Dirk and Guillermo, but maybe Dirk is staying behind to keep an eye on us. I'm eating my breakfast of oatmeal and bananas when the rain stops. The sky is still dreary and threatening.

Until now, I have not felt confined on the boat. But with

land so close, the *Sun Joule* begins to feel like a tin can. The forbidden walk between here and solid earth is only a few hundred feet, but it looks longer—bordered as it is by guardhouses and men lining the pier, their stiff posture, their straight-faces. And their oppressive, dangerous guns.

Then, Dirk steps off the boat and walks over to the guy in the guardhouse in the middle of the pier. The guard has a rifle slung over his shoulder. Maybe Dirk wants to impress him with more stories about diving with his friends in the navy. Within minutes, I see Lacey walking down the pier toward them, her ponytail high on her head, swishing behind her.

Matt said he would ask the commanding officer if Candace can take a sample of the Fouling from the piers and on the bottom of the inlet. When he and Guillermo return, he tells Candace she can take a scraping from under the pier. There will be no diving allowed in the inlet.

They have, for some reason, decided to let us go ashore while she takes her samples. The wooden pier echoes beneath our feet. How nice to walk continuously for more than 30 paces. While the others mill around at the head of the pier, I continue walking across a gravel lot. I'm so excited for the open space, I jog around this square plaza at the head of the pier. It's about the size of the parking lot at our grocery store, but it feels huge to me right now. I pick up the pace into a vigorous run until I'm sweating and panting. It feels great until I stop to stretch my unfamiliar muscles. My balance isn't quite right. After so many days on a pitching boat, the still, solid earth feels a little rocky. I nearly fall over bending down to touch my toes. I would think it's funny except for the armed guards eyeing me.

One of them approaches with an actual smile on his face. He's either laughing at me, or he feels sorry for me. Either way, his friendliness is a little disarming. He offers to let me come inside one of the stucco buildings surrounding the paved square. Says he will get me some water. I guess some of them are actually human after all.

He leads me to a metal desk and tells me to have a seat while he gets a glass. I'm looking around at the paint peeling off the cement walls when two officers walk into the room. They don't introduce themselves. "What's your name?" they ask. "Are you having a good cruise?"

"I'm Alannis," I tell him. How odd to ask about the expedition this way. As if we're on vacation. "We haven't found any Fouling, yet. But the reefs here are amazing."

The one with the round, red face sits down across from me. "And what are you looking for?" he asks. The other guy walks closer to me, reaching his bottom lip up over his mustache.

"We're looking for signs that the Fouling originated here," I tell Redface. "We can't find it yet, but in a way, that's good because when we do find it, we might be able to find out what's eating it and keeping it. . ."

Mustache man puts his hand up to stop me and walks around to stand behind me. Redface leans across the desk toward me. "No, what are YOU looking for?"

The guy with the water should be coming back soon, so I look in the direction he went.

"Your father is Dean of Braverton University, isn't that so?

"Yes..." How does this guy know that?

"He used to study, um, what was it? Marine evolutionary biology?" OK, this is getting scary. Where is the guy who was going to bring me water?

"And your mother?" It sounds more like an accusation

than a question.

"My mother is a newspaper writer." By now, I assume he already knows that.

"Not just a newspaper writer," he says, "an investigative journalist."

"Right," I stammer, "that's true."

"You must miss them, a young girl away from home so long."

Guillermo may be superstitious, but I'm starting to think he was right about the Commission's persistence. They haven't let it go. I saw the wreck, and they know it. They've been sinking ships, and I've seen the proof. Have those eyes been watching me? Reporting back to the Commission? My mind is swimming with outrageous possibilities.

"Well, we hear you've been rather unsettled."

My palms are sweating, and my throat feels parched.

"Remember, the Commission is here to protect people. We know there are stories about these waters. Stories that might capture the imagination of an inquisitive young girl such as yourself. I can assure you, they're just myths." A sucking, smacking sound over my shoulder lets me know mustache man is gumming his hairy upper lip. Finally, the smiling soldier walks in with my glass of water.

The two officers nod to him and start to leave the room. When Mustache reaches the door, he says in a soft, almost friendly voice, "We are concerned for your safety, Miss Summers. You should be very careful. Even with our protection, accidents can happen to divers in such remote locations. Especially nervous divers with overactive imaginations."

I'm not so thirsty right now. I rush out the door and find the others clustered at the head of the dock. They're ready to get back on the boat.

I need to get off this island. Why does the Commission know so much about my family? They didn't want me to come in the first place, and right now, I wish I hadn't. I wish I could talk to them.

My mother especially. She would know what to say to those men. She's navigated dangerous political situations all over the world. When I was little, and she came home after a long trip, we would almost always hear about a skirmish or coup breaking out in the city she had just left. I would crawl into her lap and cuddle up against her, waiting for the smell of her lotion to envelop me. It was the one thing I never touched when she was gone. Everything else was fair game. I washed my face with her fancy soaps, clomped around in her shoes, and played with her make-up and perfumes. But I never used her lotion. I waited for it. It was the smell of my mother safe at home.

I asked her once not to go away. She was making my lunch for school, her bags packed and waiting by the door. "Don't go this time," I pleaded. "What if it's too dangerous? What if you don't come back?"

She put down the mayonnaise-covered knife and walked around the kitchen island to face me. With both hands cradling my face she kissed my forehead. "We know what's going on in these countries. There is plenty of time to get out," she promised. "People throw around threats all the time. Mostly, it's just posturing. But we know the signs to look for when something really bad is going to happen."

In some stupid way, I want to smell her lotion right now. She would understand those Commission officers. I want her to tell me how to interpret what just happened.

CHAPTER 8

AS WE GET UNDERWAY, I STARE AT THE FACES AROUND ME for signs. The Commission knows I saw something, and someone here had to tell them. Matt and Guillermo went ashore together at first. Matt's kind of strange, and I sometimes wonder what he's doing in the lab all the time. But he's such a nerd. All he's interested in is science, board games and off-beat jokes. He's always talking about the Kraken and the spooky things that go on in the Triad. He's goofy enough that I almost think he believes in them. Plus, he seems too genuinely nice to be working with the Commission.

As for Guillermo? The Commission took him from his home, and he thought they would follow us and kill us. It hardly seems he would be on their side. I can't believe Jake would do that either. He knows I've seen things down there, but he seems more afraid of the Commission than I am. Plus, he saw the wreck, too. Dirk, on the other hand, was confident he could protect Guillermo from them. It has to be him. He was talking with the guards. But Lacey was right there with him. He didn't have time to tell them anything. Lacey would definitely tell me if Dirk had talked about me.

It doesn't make sense. None of this makes sense.

On the way out, the sky is still grey, and the water is choppy. The boat rises and falls like a rollercoaster.

It's my turn to make lunch. A quick salad and some bread

sounds easy to me, but Candace asked Guillermo to pick up calamari at the base. She wants to cook it while it's still fresh. Since I've shown her I can handle the work we're doing, she's warmed up a little. But, I'm still self conscious around her.

When I unwrap the brown paper package of calamari, I expect to see the shiny white rings that I'm used to. Instead, I find a dozen whole squid. Their bodies are about eight inches long, and their tentacles are about the same. I have never cooked calamari, and I've never seen it like this. Between that and the pitching of the boat, I'm starting to fumble around the galley.

Candace sees me staring at them and shows me how to cut off their heads and pull out the beak. On my first try, ink and brains squirt all over me. Candace drops her knife on the counter and shakes her hands at her sides with a groan. I don't get it. I deserve a little credit for tackling a pile of raw squid in a stuffy kitchen on a boat in the middle of a gut-lurching sea.

Candace never groans or pinches her lips into a stern disapproving face at Lacey, even though Lacey sometimes acts like a girly drama queen—not the intelligent scientist she really is. And she doesn't roll her eyes at Matt's weird jokes or Dirk's obnoxious stories. In fact, she not only asks for their opinions, she seems to actually like them. What do I have to do to prove myself to Dr. Warren?

It's Candace's recipe of course, but I feel pretty satisfied when everyone Oohs and Aaahs at the lunch we spread out on the galley counter. The first thing Matt does is pick up a long tentacle and say, "Don't worry, my little baby kraken, your mama's coming to get us all." Matt has turned the kraken into a running joke since he first brought it up.

When Lacey and Dirk come into the salon for lunch, they tell us what they heard from one of the guards this morning.

"The Fouling is still spreading north," Dirk says.

"It's covering almost ten miles a day in some areas," Lacey adds.

That's almost unbelievable. Nothing moves that fast. The Fouling doesn't spread like a vine taking over a forest. They think it spreads like a dandelion, dispersing millions of microscopic eggs that grow into some kind of larvae which drift on the currents. When they find something solid to attach to, they settle out into a red slime and rapidly grow into black crust. That's what they think happens. But, no matter how hard they've tried, no one has been able to collect Fouling eggs or larvae. It's baffling, but there is no other way miles of coastline can become covered in Fouling overnight.

"Three oil tankers and a cargo ship are also missing in the Atlantic," Lacey says. "Every country with a port to the Atlantic Ocean is talking about shutting down shipping traffic."

Matt whistles the eerie tune he made up to go along with his jokes about the Triad, but it falls flat. This is serious news. Almost everything bought or sold around the world comes from someplace else. If shipping stopped, things would fall apart. No fuel. No supplies. No parts to keep things running. In some places, there would be no food.

No food. It doesn't even seem possible, and I think of the pantry back home. Are my parents stocking up?

The next morning, when I drag myself out of bed, everyone else is just finishing breakfast. Sully and Jake have already been in to clean the bottom. Sully says there was only a bit of algae, but Jake insists it's slimier and thicker than what he's seen in the past. He thinks it might be important to look at it more closely, but the rest of the team won't sit down and listen to him.

They dismissed him before, too, when he took Guillermo's place as Matt's dive partner. He rattled off a few things he saw, and although Matt seemed genuinely interested, the rest of them didn't pay much attention. They make it obvious he's not a part of the scientific team.

Although the storm has passed, the water is still a little choppy. The waves are stirring up silt from the bottom. "Visibility is pretty low from the turbulence," Sully announces.

"We'll be diving close to the boat" Candace says, "No long-distance forays. We're on the edge of a blackout zone, so let's not stray too far."

She goes in first. Not far behind her, I press my mask to my face and step off the dive platform. As soon as the bubbles clear, I realize that in the Caribbean, what passes for low visibility is considered normal back home. I'm used to murky water, so this shouldn't bother me. But I'm tired, and something about this place puts me on edge. I feel that mysterious presence behind me again.

I'm looking around for the Fouling when I hear a *clang, clang, clang.* Candace is tapping the bottom of her scuba tank with her knife. She wants me to come see something.

There it is. A ribbon of black cement-like crust about six inches wide and three feet long, snaking its way between two brain corals. She removes a small lead cylinder from a clip on her BC, and unwinds the thin rope wrapped around it. She ties the rope to an orange bag, then fills the bag with air. When she lets go, the bag floats to the surface. Her marker buoy is set. We swim quickly back to the boat.

Candace doesn't want to wait for everyone else to return, so as soon as we have our tanks off, she gathers up the camera, a 30-foot measuring tape on a spool, a plastic slate to write on, and some Ziploc bags for samples. Her plan is to return to our marker buoy and dive back down to the patch of Fouling. She's going to photograph, measure, and take notes, while I swim out with the spool of measuring tape. When I get to the end, I'll weigh it down and send up another marker buoy.

On my way back to Candace, I'm supposed to note how many patches of Fouling I find—if any—and estimate their size for later measurements. Unless the others have seen Fouling, the whole team will probably spend the rest of the day surveying this small area of reef.

It probably takes less than twenty minutes to gather everything up and discuss our plan before plunging back in the water. I keep my game face on, but inside, I'm jumping up and down wildly. This is what I came for, and now it's happening. I think about what this really means. *I was there when Candace Warren found the Fouling. I helped her solve the problem.*

I reach the end of the tape and clip a weight around it. As soon as I let go of the weight, I start to rise off the bottom, so I dump some air out of my BC and sink back down. Visibility is low enough that Candace is just a blurry shadow beneath a white cloud of rising bubbles. I'm trying to pull an orange bag from my gear net when a vague shadow dims the seafloor around me. A tingle crawls up my spine. Something is definitely behind me. I freeze, unsure what I should do. My breath catches and my regulator goes silent.

With a deep breath, I turn to face an expanse of empty water. There's nothing there. The reef slopes down toward a sharp ledge that looks like a drop off, but I can't tell. Something big darts away in the distance. It's hanging in the water beyond the ledge. A dark shadow moving slowly in the murky water.

If this is the thing we all felt behind us on the first few

dives, I have to know what it is. I think of the officers back at the base. "Accidents can happen." I think of the shipwreck Jake and I saw. We're on the border of a blackout zone, but we're not IN one. If Candace hadn't seen the Fouling, we would have swum right to the edge of this drop off anyway. If I can just get a little closer to this fish, or whatever it is, I can get a clearer view. I would love to be able to tell everyone I identified that mysterious presence we all felt.

I have a 50-foot rope that I'm supposed to use for my marker buoy, so I weigh it down next to my tape measure and begin to unwind it as I swim toward the ridge. With this low visibility, I could easily get confused on my way back and end up looking around for my tape measure. I'll just swim a short distance to see, then follow my rope back.

I'm going deeper, and the pressure is building in my ears. I pinch my nose and swallow until they clear. I should glance at my computer to check my depth, but I don't want to take my eyes off that thing in the distance. I'm afraid it will dart and I'll lose it. I'm nearing the end of my rope and it isn't any clearer. It must be farther away than I thought. The drop off is directly in front of me. Below that, darkness.

Whatever it was, it's gone now. I strain my eyes harder. Nothing.

Oh my god.

Those eyes are right there. Right in front of me! Out of nowhere. For a millisecond I'm paralyzed as my brain adjusts to the signals my eyes are sending it. A face, two eyes, a whole body. And it's a foot away!

A switch flips on somewhere inside me and sends a bolt of lightning through me. I try to swim backwards as my flailing arms and legs stir up sand and bits of broken coral. I turn myself around and kick back up the slope as fast as I can. I've dropped the line, but pure instinct brings me back to my spot at the end of the tape measure. My legs burn from the swim. I can't catch my breath. A part of my brain calls to me through the panic. *Breathe out, slow down, watch your diving.* All my training kicks in. *Don't bolt to the surface. Bolting is bad. Don't bolt.*

I look back but can't see anything below. Candace's white cloud of bubbles in the distance is immediately reassuring. I swim toward them where she is positioning the camera on a stand over the coral. She's focusing and doesn't look at me. I want to go, but I can't just grab her. Being next to another person feels just a little bit safer. *Be calm, I tell myself. Breathe. Wait.*

Something taps my shoulder, and I'm paralyzed with fear. Then it moves around to face me.

It's him.

I see all of him. Blue and green. A face with practically no nose, round black eyes, and. . . and a shimmering tail. He stretches out a hand. . . a HAND. In it is my rope, neatly wrapped into a ball. He tilts his head to the side and pushes the ball of rope toward me. My hand automatically lifts to take it.

He's gone. Like that. I took the ball, and he disappeared, leaving only a streak of tiny bubbles in the water.

Candace touches my arm, and I snap back to reality. She holds her palms up to ask, "What?" I fight the panic welling up in me. I'm on auto-pilot, handing her the ball of rope. I don't really know what my body is doing, but I have to get to the surface. I lift my dive computer and move my fingertips back and forth in front of my throat. The sign for out of air. She looks at me as if I'm crazy, and I point a thumb to the surface. "Up," I'm telling her.

The boat is a silhouette above us, and we slowly make our way toward it. It's all I can do to control my ascent. On the way, I think about the risks of panicking. How deep did I go? I was only down a second? Was it safe? Did I hold my breath? Will I have an embolism? Will I get decompression sickness? I should go slowly. I don't wait for Candace to get out of the water first.

I drop my gear on the bench. Everything is spinning. My stomach feels squeezed into my throat. I run as far forward as I can before I collapse across the rail and throw up.

Oh my god. This can't be real. This doesn't happen. Hanging over the rail, I pick up my head to look out at the ocean. It's still spinning. I feel Jake's hands on my shoulders, and everything goes white.

CHAPTER 9

WHEN I WAKE, JAKE IS HOLDING MY HEAD IN HIS LAP. I'M still along the side between the cabin and the rail. I don't want to look up. I don't want to see the water. I want to be in bed, at home, on land.

Candace and Sully peer at me over Jake's shoulders. "Alannis, are you all right? What happened?" Candace urges me to tell her I'm OK.

I look up at Jake and then at her and Sully. What can I say? This isn't real. I can't come out and say, "I saw a fishman." I close my eyes and lie there breathing for a little while.

Jake asks, "Did you take the sea-sickness pills I gave you this morning?"

I have no idea what he means, but I shake my head no. "No," I moan, "no, no, no," and it feels good to let something out. *No this isn't happening,* I want to scream.

Candace wipes my hair away from my face. "Come on. Let's get you some water." As I stand up, I feel foolish. I have an urge to defend myself.

"I don't get seasick," I blurt out, "I never get seasick."

"It's OK. It happens," Sully says.

Behind us, Lacey and Matt are just getting back on deck. "Please don't tell them," I beg.

Candace whispers, "Shh, it's OK. We don't have to say

anything." In contrast to her normal coolness, Candace's compassion feels both comforting and embarrassing.

As we walk into the salon, Sully begins a story about one of their former dive instructors. "She was one of our best divers, but as soon as it got a little choppy, Kim got sick. Remember that, Jake? She'd help her whole class suit up and tell them to wait for her on the platform. They'd just be hanging out there while she'd be in the head chucking up her last meal."

"Dad," Jake implores, and it's the first time I've heard him call Sully Dad.

"Really, she would. But then she'd march right on back there and jump in with her class." Sully throws me a gentle smile and adds, "Every time."

Half a bottle of water later, I manage to make my mouth work. Once again, I'm angry that Jake's quick cover story makes me look like a fool. But on the other hand, I'm also grateful I don't have to try to explain what just happened. "I'm fine," I tell them. "I think I had too much for breakfast. Maybe I'm coming down with something. I don't know, but can I go lie down in my cabin?" Dirk and Guillermo must be up by now, and I want to get down there quickly. I don't want to deal with Dirk again.

In the cabin, with the door closed, I collapse on Lacey's bunk, shaking. I have no idea how to deal with this. There ARE no underwater things that look like people and have fish tails and roll rope into balls with actual hands. They don't exist. My stomach lurches as if I just plunged from the top of a rollercoaster. I throw myself at the vanity sink and throw up again.

Oh my god, what am I going to do with this information? As if the whole world just turned upside-down, there is no ground under my feet. I have never wanted to be on land so badly. I wish I were anywhere but here, doing anything but this. I need to touch something I know is real, something from home. I remember my fuzzy slippers and dig them out from the bottom of my locker. I hold them tightly curled under my chin.

*

I don't know how I got onto my bunk, or how long I've been here, but the knock on the door sends me shooting head first into the ceiling. "Ow! Come in."

It's Jake; he tells me everyone thinks he's up in the wheelhouse with Sully who thinks he's back on deck with everyone else.

"Thanks for the rundown," I croak, realizing he wants me to know that he's trying not to be seen with me.

"What was it?" he demands. His tanned face takes on an angry red tint and he fixes his icy blue eyes on mine without flinching. This aggression is shocking after the way he held my head in his lap. "What happened down there?"

I want to tell him. I don't want to hold on to this terrifying secret all alone. I picture myself explaining it. I rehearse it quickly in my head. *I saw a man down there. He had a tail instead of legs, and he wrapped up my rope and gave it to me.* I just can't make the words out loud. Jake sits on the edge of the vanity with one foot propped on Lacey's bunk. He leans forward, pressing me to answer.

"Something spooked you bad. This is the second time, now. Does this have anything to do with what we saw on our swim?"

A tight knot begins to form deep in my gut. My voice flattens as I say, "I don't know. It was hard to tell. Maybe it was nothing."

"Well, you're the only one who keeps coming back with something to hide." He's not being mean exactly, but he's making no effort to comfort me. Clearly, he's more interested in making sure I don't rock the boat. "I saw your dive computer, Alannis. What were you doing at 70 feet?"

Seventy feet? I had no idea I had gone that deep.

"Don't worry, I cleared your computer," he says in a scalding tone. My Computer! I hadn't even thought about how I would explain my depth to Dirk if he decided to check. I should thank Jake for trying to help, but the fear welling up in my throat spills out of my mouth like an accusation.

"You can't clear a computer," I say. "The dive data's still there."

"You can clear it if you know how," he answers just under his breath. I open my mouth to argue, but his expression tells me to drop it. "I won't cover for you anymore," he barks. "If you're going off looking for something, you're on your own. This is no joke, Alannis. Stay out of whatever it is."

He stands and leaves me alone again.

Pull yourself together, I tell myself. *You're still alive. Our boat is still here. Everybody's safe.* That creature didn't hurt me. He gave me back my rope and kind of smiled. No, that's crap. He didn't smile. And he wasn't a person. He was a mutant fish, or something. Some horrible, wretched experiment from the days of Barru Pi. Maybe I'm exaggerating. Or imagining. I've been on edge this whole trip. There's no way I saw what I think I saw.

But, I did.

The cabin door opens without a knock, and Sully walks in. "Hey there." He tilts his chin up and affects an English accent. "Dinner is being served on the upper deck." With the word "dinner," my stomach lurches. Have I been here all day?

I missed the afternoon dives? I missed lunch. "You don't look so good. Are you OK there, missy?"

"Yeah, I'm a little queasy still."

"Well, nerves can do that on a boat, you know. Even if you don't usually get seasick." He looks so much older than my father, more like a grandfather. "You looked pretty shaken this morning; anything happen down there?"

I remember what Jake said. About how I remind Sully of his daughter. It makes me want a hug from him. I want to tell him everything. But then, it doesn't feel right. He'll think I'm crazy. Besides, he has even more to lose than Jake does if something messes up this cruise. I shake my head, unable to get any words out.

"Sure?" he says.

"I'm good," I lie. "Really, I think I ate too much this morning before diving in that chop."

"OK then, you should get some fresh air." He pats my knee.

"I'll be there in five. I'm going to change first." As I jump down from my bunk, the damp bedding reminds me that I haven't even changed out of my bathing suit. My skin is grainy and itchy with salt from the seawater.

When I join the team, I sit at the settee, listening numbly to everyone talk about the afternoon dives. Jake apparently took my place as Candace's dive buddy, and he rattles off the names of endangered fish, and coral, and invertebrates he saw down there.

Candace has finally heard him. She gives him a look of surprise. "You sure know your species."

"Been diving a long time," he says.

"You should consider doing something with your interests," she says. "Perhaps you should think about pursuing a college degree."

"You can learn a lot as a tour guide," Dirk adds, "but you'll need to go to school if you want to do more than that." My eyes bug out of my head. They're making such false assumptions, and Jake isn't even speaking up. Why doesn't he tell them he had his pick of any school he wanted? It's none of my business, but I'm furious with him. I want him to stand up and defend himself.

Just then, Guillermo remarks on the diversity of little bottom-hopping fish called blennies. He says half of them must be species no one has ever seen before. Matt adds that every time one of the researchers in his new lab dives in the mangroves off Honduras, she finds at least one new species of *Littorina*, a periwinkle. One is even named after him. I can imagine that. *Littorina weirdus-mattensis*, the snail.

Over dinner my stomach settles a little. I'm thankful no one presses me about how I feel. I go to the bow to lie on my back and watch the purples and pinks of twilight melt into deep indigo. What could that thing have been? Could it really be some mutant creature Barru Pi created? Some man with arms, and hands, two round black eyes, and a tail with flukes? His skin was iridescent and his face oddly shaped. Already, I'm having trouble picturing him exactly. He wasn't a fish at all, but he wasn't quite a man.

Maybe this thing is natural. We've discovered new species all over these reefs, and the islands have been so remote for so long. It's hard to believe, but it's not impossible. Marine mammals did evolve from land mammals after all.

I understood that the first time I learned how evolution worked. I was five. My dad and I were throwing stones into the waves back home when we found the remains of a baby seal in the surf. We rolled the seal over with Dad's flip-flop. The head was gone. One of its flippers—stripped of flesh—revealed bones that looked just like the hands on my brother's glow-in-the-dark skeleton pj's. "It has hands?" I asked my dad. "No," he said, "but you can tell it had feet once." I thought he meant the little seal was born with feet. But my dad kept explaining. It was the most amazing thing I had ever heard. "Whales and dolphins, all of them used to have legs and feet. They lived on land until one day, a long, long time ago, they crawled into the sea and learned to swim." I remember asking if they had to wear swimmies. He told me their legs and feet eventually shrank and became fins, because fins were more useful than feet underwater. I wanted to take the baby seal's bones home with us, but he pinched his nose and said they were too stinky.

He let me poke at it with a stick. A huge chunk of its side was missing. "Shark attack," my father said dryly. I dug around in the crescent-shaped void of the bite mark until my father grabbed my wrist. I thought he was angry and wanted me to stop, but he had seen something, a dime-sized jaggedy shark tooth. Gingerly, he pulled it out with two fingers and presented it to me. The next Valentine's Day, he gave me an ankle bracelet, and I have worn that tooth as a charm ever since. Before I left home, I took it off and put it on my dresser. I thought it might look childish to wear a good luck charm. Now, as I sit up and pull my knees into my chest, my ankles feel bare.

Sully finds me on the bow and sits cross-legged next to me. He tells me I'm clearly still out of sorts and wants to know if it's something more than seasickness. "Did something spook you on your dive?" he asks paternally. I shake my head no. Anything I say will sound unconvincing. "It's a stressful time for everyone," he says. "I suppose the fish that no one can see and Guillermo's legends might be taking a toll, young lady."

I shrug, afraid to open my mouth. After a few minutes of silence, I ask him, "Sully, was Dirk right? Can the navy train marine mammals?"

Sully looks surprised. "Is that what's scaring you?" he asks. "What Dirk said? What would make you think of that?"

"Do you think Barru Pi could have had something like that?" I ask him. "A guard or something to watch people who come near the islands?"

"Why? Did you see something?" he asks.

"It's just that—" I stumble here, wondering how much to say. "We've all felt something right? Something watching us? What about Guillermo's legends? Those perrorap things? Do you think they could be real?"

"Ah, yes, giant squid that eat sailors," Sully says with a sigh that sounds like relief. "The legends of an island people and their magical dictators. You better believe monsters like that would keep me in line if I were a Cubbarran. Remember, legends are sometimes meant to distract people from seeing the truth.

"Look," he takes a Swiss army knife from his pocket and unties from it a thin rope. At the other end, the rope is knotted into a small cube, a monkey's fist. "You see this little knot, right?" He holds it up in his palm. Then he waves his other hand over it. The knot remains in his palm. "No magic," he says, "right?"

"Right," I nod. You're kidding me. He's going to do one of those corny sleight of hand tricks that I'm supposed to giggle over, as if that will suddenly make everything better.

"Do you believe I'm going to make the knot disappear?" he asks, curling his fingers around the monkey's fist and waves it around my head. "Well, if I can control what you believe, then I can get away with whatever I want. Now, reach into your pocket." Somehow, his knife is there. I'm amazed, and for just a second, I'm not thinking about underwater creatures.

"Don't worry about Guillermo's sea monsters." Sully pats my knee and winks. "I have powerful magic of my own to keep them away."

Sully groans his way up to a standing position. "Of course, the Commission is another story. No joking around there. We'd just better keep our eyes open and our noses out of places they don't belong, right?"

I nod, and hold his pocket knife up to him.

"Keep it, sweetie. You just let me know if something scares you," he says. "You can talk to me anytime."

I turn his knife over in my hand. He's wrong. I can't talk to anyone about this.

CHAPTER 10

YESTERDAY, WHILE I WAS SHAKING IN MY CABIN, THE TEAM placed screen enclosures over the patch of Fouling to keep fish from grazing on it. They want to see if that's what's keeping it in check. They collected samples of it for slides, and they put a big chunk of it in a plastic tub near the dive platform. They're trying to keep it alive by pumping fresh seawater over it through some hoses they hung over the back of the boat. This is actually beginning to look like a research trip. Candace and Matt are staying in the lab this morning to look at the slides under a microscope. The rest of us are going down to continue surveying the area.

I don't want to go in at all. That thing is going to be watching us. I tell them I still feel a little weak from yesterday. It sounds like a wimpy excuse, and Candace tilts her head toward Jake. "You're up," she says indifferently.

While Jake prepares his gear, I mull over the consequences of staying back. Jake knows all these reef species by their Latin names. He's probably as steady and meticulous underwater as he is on deck. Meanwhile, the circumstances haven't helped me shine.

I don't want to ruin things for him, and I kind of feel bad about this, but I have to dive. The last thing I want is for him to outdo me. I assume I'll be paired with Lacey, but I'm not that lucky. When I step in and tell Jake I'm up, Dirk tells me we'll buddy up. Lacey looks just as disappointed as I am. She's diving with Guillermo.

On our way down, I search the water in all directions. It's clear today, and fish of all sizes swim and dart and float in abundance. I stay as close to Dirk as I can without seeming strange. He stays right next to me. He breathes slowly, and I metre my breaths to the sound of his bubbles. It has a calming effect.

As we swim toward our patch of Fouling, Dirk points to a large grouper tucked into an alcove. It's maybe three feet long. I look and nod. OK, whatever, it's a grouper. True, it might seem huge in most places, but it's a baby compared to some of the ones we've seen down here. Then he points to its gaping mouth. I hadn't noticed the shrimp inside. I stop to watch it, and hear the *click-click* noises it makes as it cleans parasites from the fish's mouth. Dirk's gesture reminds me how marvelous this place is. Oddly, I feel safer in the water with Dirk than I did with Candace.

When we get to the patch of Fouling the team found yesterday, we work shoulder to shoulder identifying coral and algae, and taking notes. Yesterday, the team ran string in a grid pattern over the Fouling and surrounding reef. Dirk and I will stay in this one spot the entire dive, surveying 20-centimeter squares of our two-meter grid. The Fouling skirts along the base of a Barrel sponge so large I could climb inside. It blocks the view to my left, and no matter how hard I try to keep my mind on our work, I'm afraid the marine mammal man will lunge out at me from behind the sponge.

I've finished one square, and the next one is filled with something I don't recognize. A cluster of delicate white discs on long thin stalks. They're cupped into shallow bowls with spoke-like ridges stretching out from the center. I've never seen this before, so I tap Dirk on the shoulder and point to it. He takes my dive slate and my pencil and scribbles *Acetabularia– mermaid's wineglass*. While he's writing I watch behind him, looking quickly from side to side. Making sure nothing comes at us out of nowhere. Maybe I'm breathing quickly, or maybe I look as nervous as I am, but out of nowhere, Dirk decides he needs to take charge.

He puts his fingers up in a "V" shape. He points to my eyes, and then his. "Look at me," his hands say. He grips his regulator hose close to his mouth and takes a deep breath. "Breathe," his little display is telling me. We're kneeling on the bottom, face to face. He puts his left hand on my shoulder and takes a deep breath in. Then he takes the regulator out of his mouth and breathes out a steady stream of glassy bubbles. He puts his regulator back in. Takes a slow breath and does it again. This is a test, and I'm meant to follow along. So, I lock my eyes onto his and take up his lead. Regulator out. Breathe out slow and steady. Regulator in. Breathe in.

This is what dive instructors do when they train a newbie. In his drill sergeant way Dirk is trying to make sure I'm calm and in control. I watch his eyes through two more rounds until I'm ready to laugh. I'm reminded of a scout master taking himself too seriously. All he needs is a crisp khaki uniform and shiny new badges.

We put our regulators back in our mouths, and he puts up the OK sign. It's a question. "OK," my hand answers back.

Throughout the dive, as he measures and writes, I can feel his attention on me. I'm very careful to monitor my breathing. I don't know what I'm more concerned about, seeing that thing again, or proving to Dirk I'm a good diver. His attention is menacing, but I have to admit that it's comforting to know he is watching out for me.

A shadow moves over us, and my body tenses. I cringe, and fight the urge to whip my head around. Dirk touches my elbow and points overhead. A pair of sea turtles is barreling down on us. They buzz right by, their fins touching down, kicking up sand and clumps of debris before clumsily crawling and paddling their way back into the water column. They're playful and beautiful. Dirk nods at me with wide eyes. If he didn't have that regulator sticking out of his mouth, I would swear he was laughing.

He looks over to one side and points at a trumpet fish. It's a funny looking fish, long and skinny with a trumpet-shaped mouth. Time and again, we take a break to watch something amazing swim by. But it's never what I'm looking for.

We're almost finished surveying our grids when Dirk tugs on my arm and points to a mound of reef in front of us. I hear his muffled voice saying, "Look, look." A moray eel swims freely in the water. I usually only see them peering out from inside a crevice or under a ledge of coral. Their prehistoric heads sway at the entrances to their lairs, their long jaws open and full of razor sharp teeth. Around morays, divers are careful not to wear silver watches or anything that might look like a flashy silver fish. They're lightning fast, and pack a vicious bite. This one must be ten feet long. It's bigger and brighter than any eel I've ever seen. It's patterned like a giraffe with brown spots over green and purple skin. Dirk and I hover in the water next to each other, watching until it disappears, an iridescent ribbon sailing gracefully over the reef. Underwater, this is a whole different Dirk.

Unfortunately it doesn't last. When we get back on deck, he snaps back to the old Dirk, watching everyone put their gear away and telling us how long a break we need before we can dive again.

For the next two days, there is no sign of that marine mammal man. Anxiously, I look for him everywhere. Half of me is afraid he will show up. Half of me wants to see him. While I watch for him, Dirk watches me like a hawk. If my breathing quickens, he looks at me. If I turn to look at something in the distance, he follows my gaze, and he watches me. That simple fact is comforting in a way. But mostly, it's annoying. I really don't like him.

After ten dives with him, I have given him my own private nick name. "Dive Sergeant Jerk Peterson." Fortunately, I don't have to listen to his long brag fests about dangerous diving adventures. Lacey bears the brunt of most of that when he follows her up to the bow. Every day, hovering around her. Above water, I don't know how anybody can stand him. When we're all in the salon, and he launches one of his stories, I find something that needs to be done. I take an extra turn in the galley, or I retreat to the lab and try to make myself useful. Even with all of Matt's creepy talk about the kraken and the Triad, it's better than hanging around Dirk.

Yesterday, Matt showed me the slides of the Fouling. What Candace collected off the pilings in Cubbarros is exactly the same Fouling we have at home. But what we're collecting on the reef is slightly different. Under the microscope, the long hard tubes that make up the crust have fewer branches than the Fouling. It may be a variant, or a completely different species. They can't do genetic testing here, but they know it's not the same Fouling.

Not only is there something keeping it from spreading here, but this variant may simply not be as aggressive. Sully let Candace use the satellite phone to report this new finding to the university. The news from home is growing worse every day. The Fouling is accelerating. Shipping ports have been crippled, and the only shipping routes still operating are the ones in the cold waters of the North. The shortage of oil and gas is becoming critical. All up and down the coast, wherever the Fouling has been seen, fishing has stopped. Fish plants shut down. Seafood restaurants closed. Boat businesses gone. So many people are fleeing areas devastated by the Fouling, they're like refugees flooding the rest of the country. There's no work for them.

Candace didn't ask how things were going in New England. Or if she did, she wouldn't say. Could this be affecting them at home yet? I have a sudden image of tents filled with refugees on our front lawn. The university campus would be overrun first. The quad, a huge open space where students gather to study and play Frisbee and soccer, would make a perfect place for a tent city.

Candace tells us there have been riots all over North and South America. The Fouling is a disaster. If it keeps up, we're headed for a global depression that could be more devastating than anything in human history.

.

CHAPTER 11

I'VE SPENT MOST OF TODAY IN THE LAB LOOKING OVER Matt's shoulder and trying to avoid everyone else. Matt's beginning to grow on me. I never feel like I have to prove myself to him. He's so nonjudgmental. True, he looks at everything with a sick, dark humor. But it's the only humor on the boat right now, and I'll take it.

Before dinner, Lacey finds me in the lab putting the equipment away. "Where have you been? You're like a total worker bee around here."

"I'm here to work," I tell her, "and, to be honest, sometimes I need a break from Dirk. He's just so intense. And all of his stories. . ." I expect her to sigh with a big "Ugh" and say something like, "I know what you mean."

Instead she says, "I love his stories. You know, he's dived in almost every ocean." Her voice has the bubbly lilt of infatuation. "He has really good taste in music, too." She digs her tablet out from her locker, and pulls up an album. *Running in Circles* by Insomnia. Not my favorite. Too much of a pop band trying to sound like a rock band. "This is Dirk's favorite song. Mine too. Don't you love it?"

"Sure," I lie. "But he seems more classic rock to me. I really can't imagine him singing along to Insomnia."

Lacey takes a wide-legged stance and rolls her shoulders back. She holds her elbows away from her body as if her muscles were just too big for her to hold them any closer. Then she sings a refrain in a really low voice. "*You got me runnin' runnin' runnin' You got me chasin' you 'round again. I'm fallin' fallin' fallin'. Dizzy in love with you.*" Surprisingly, she's nailed Dirk, and we both crack up. So, Lacey totally gets it. Now it makes even less sense that she actually likes him.

"Underneath all that bravado," she says, "he's a nice guy. He's really concerned about you. He's asked me a couple of times if you're OK, and if something is bothering you on the dives." Sure, he's concerned. He doesn't want me to have a dive accident on his watch.

"He sure hides it well," I tell her.

"He's very observant, Alannis, and he does care. He's the reason we got to stretch our legs a little at the base. He was thinking of you."

OK, she's got my attention now. Keep going.

"He told the guards he thought you were a little homesick. He thought you might enjoy some time away from the boat."

I'm stunned. "What else did he say?"

"Nothing, just that you've been kind of skittish on the dives, afraid of your shadow, you know. And you have to admit, you spend a lot of time alone up on the bow, listening to those creepy sad whales and monkeys."

For a doctor who's probably ten years older than me, I can't believe Lacey is that stupid! "Lacey, he's with the Commission! He thinks I know about something."

Lacey's laughing wholeheartedly at me. "Where did you get that idea?"

"From you. You said it yourself the first night." I'm about to tell her how he's been watching me since Jake and I went swimming, but I think I've said too much already.

"I did? Well, whatever. Don't take that kind of stuff seriously. He does look like one, but that doesn't mean he is. Candace asked him to come. He was her graduate student. He's like, THE expert in invasive species dispersal patterns."

I'm not as convinced as she is. Sometimes he acts as if he's in command, and he always wants to know what everyone on the boat is doing. Lacey is too distracted to see the truth. I might as well assume from now on that whatever I tell her will get right back to Dirk.

At dinner I'm bothered by the feeling I can't trust anyone. We're sitting on the top deck, and I'm only half listening as the scientists discuss how the Cubbarros crust differs from the Fouling. Candace and Matt think we found the same thing the Spanish explorer described in his reports 300 years ago. It's what has been living here harmlessly all these years.

"Obviously, we must be dealing with a variant," Candace says.

"A much more aggressive variant," Matt ads. "If the Fouling that's taking over the coastlines comes from here, it must have recently adapted to take advantage of oil spills."

"Could be," Lacey says "If that's the case, the new Fouling may have no natural predators. It would be impossible to contain."

Sully jumps up and grabs the binos out of the wheelhouse. "Boats," he says, surprising all of us. There shouldn't be other boats out here. But tiny lights wink on the eastern horizon. "Looks like submarines."

Dirk is on his feet, his hands grabbing for Sully's binoculars. Sully hands them over, and Dirk holds them to his eyes for a few seconds. "They're out there all right. Nuclear. Only other vessels likely to risk it. No oil, no Fouling."

"It appears someone wants to keep an eye on us,"

Candace says. "I'm surprised they weren't here sooner."

Guillermo takes his turn with the binos. "They are Commission," he says. "OSC-TK4s. You can see clearly their outline." I can't see much of anything very clearly except another cluster of twinkling lights beyond the bow to the north. "Look, more subs," I say.

Guillermo follows my pointing finger with the binos until Dirk snatches them away.

"Navy," he announces. "Dorado class attack sub."

"We're pretty darn close to that blackout zone," Sully says. "I'll bet the Commission is just keeping an eye on us. Protecting their space, you know."

"Or reminding us not to cross the line again," Matt ads.

Candace tears her eyes away from the lights to look at Matt. "And I suspect the Navy may be here to keep an eye on us as well. To ensure the Commission does not cross any lines either."

"To protect us," Guillermo chuckles. "To protect this important mission. Yes. Perhaps."

We finish dinner with awkward conversation about what their arrival means. So far, the Commission has been able to track our every move with the transponders on our antenna. Why they would suddenly want to hover in the distance is not clear, but the submarines aren't threatening us, and they can't reach us directly. The reef is too shallow and dangerous for them. Maybe they're waiting for us to make another mistake— like go swimming with the captain's son in the blackout zone and find another ship wreck we're not supposed to see.

Maybe Guillermo was right when he said they would watch us. Another move like that and they might kill us all. The navy subs hovering nearby make me feel safer, but only slightly. The image of that sunken ship rising from the bottom worries me.

When Dirk excuses himself to go fill tanks, I'm about to get up and join him. The thought of it sours my stomach, but it's still my duty. Lacey jumps in front of me. "I'll go fill the tanks if you want a break." She's definitely infatuated. Along with telling me Dirk was an agent, didn't she tell me a dive boat is a romantic place?

Everyone leaves, but Guillermo and Candace. It's a beautiful night. The whales have started singing. Guillermo's accent is almost musical, and I want to stay to listen to him. I'm not even paying attention to the words, just the rhythm. It's a little awkward, but they don't seem to mind that I'm there. Candace and Guillermo often sit up here together for hours—discussing their work, I guess.

As darkness falls, lights from the submarines sparkle in the distance like a constellation of red and white stars. We watch them in silence. Guillermo lights a cigar and lets out a long exhale. "I worry, Candace. They are a troublesome sign." The melody of his voice has changed.

"What do you think they are watching for?" Candace asks. I tense my shoulders and hope he doesn't look at me.

"They have come when you reported this new finding. The variation in the Fouling," he answers, his eyes fixed on the cigar as he rolls it between his fingers. "I worry more perhaps that your Navy has come. For them, this mutation is not a good thing, my friend. It will be too easy to assume it was intentional."

"What do you mean?" Candace asks.

"Engineered. Genetically altered for a reason."

"A biological weapon?" she says with shock. "Guillermo, there is no evidence of that."

"Evidence does not matter," he answers. "What matters is

what people believe. The world believed that Barru Pi poisoned her island and her people. It would not be hard for them to believe she created the Fouling. They would want the islands destroyed in revenge. "

"That would be extreme, don't you think?" Candace says.

"The Fouling is extreme. This plague, it is devastating," Guillermo argues. "There are many, many victims. And victims need someone to blame for their suffering."

"You think the Cubbarros Islands will become the scapegoat?"

"It is convenient, no?" He stares in the direction of the submarines. "These islands are abandoned dots on a map. Wipe the plague away with a bomb or two and be done with the memory of Barru Pi and her people forever."

So far, I have tried to remain the observant fly on the wall, but I can't help but blurt out, "They wouldn't do that!"

Guillermo continues to look out over the black horizon. "A tiny island nation?" he says, although it has not been a nation for many decades. "It would not be so hard to destroy. How many bombs does your navy's small armada of submarines carry? Our island, our beautiful reefs, all of it gone."

"But that wouldn't stop the Fouling," I protest.

"It would stop the riots," he says with a tired exhale. "A common enemy will unite the angry masses. At least for a while. It would turn the anger this way."

"I don't believe the Navy would want to do that," Candace says, "The Commission would fight them."

"Perhaps, yes," he says. "But then the world would have a bigger enemy to unite against, and a lengthy battle to distract them."

"A war with the Commission," she whispers almost to

herself. "An excuse to slay the dragon."

"Barru Pi or the Commission. No matter which dragon they choose," he replies, barely audible, "Cubbarros will be destroyed."

Candace and Guillermo fall into silence. I wonder which of the lights in the distance belong to the Commission and which to the Navy.

It's probably not even 10:00, but it feels late. I excuse myself to go to bed. I'm trying to sort out everything that's happened since I've been on this boat. Is Dirk an agent or not? Did he tell the Commission I saw the wreck? Did I see a new species or a mutant creature left over from Barru Pi's experiments? Could that be where the legend of the perrorap came from? Does the Commission know about it? Or worse, is the Commission training it?

Will I ever see it again?

CHAPTER 12

LACEY HAS BEEN IN HER BUNK SLEEPING FOR WHAT FEELS like hours. Her breathing is deep and steady. With the gentle rocking of the boat, the hollow sound of water slapping easily against the hull, I should be deep in sleep myself by now. All of the reasons that brought me here seem both pointless and naïve. The Fouling is more than an environmental crisis, more than just biology gone haywire. Our chances of stopping it dwindle by the day. What's more, we're at the center of a political struggle that may not only lead to a war, but possibly destroy an entire chain of islands and reefs—one of the few untouched, idyllic natural environments left in the world.

With all this stuff going on, I worry about what's happening back home. Is everything already falling apart there, too? I'm ashamed to think this way, but if the Fouling can't survive in cold water, this disaster is still something happening to other people, not to me. I'm not proud of these thoughts, but this is not what I expected from the expedition. I wanted to work with a famous scientist, do real underwater science, solve a major environmental problem, launch my dream career. If I have to admit it, I liked the idea of spending a couple of months scuba diving while everyone else back home was bearing the drudgery of high school.

That seems petty now. What I wouldn't do for that drudgery. Oh, how I wish I were completely ignorant of all of this. I wish all those desperate, displaced people on TV wandering everywhere looking for work and food and homes were still just shadows to me. Masses who had nothing to do with me, could never touch me, were not fully real.

But they are real. And even if the Fouling never reaches as far north as Braverton Bay—even if my own home and family can stay safe from it—Jake and Sully are just one job away from being those people. When this project ends, where will they go?

I don't want to think about any of this. The moon breaks through my porthole and shines across me like the beam of a flashlight. This cabin feels like a coffin. I want off this boat. I get out of bed, put on my shorts and a hoodie, and go up on deck. I feel the breeze on my face. Stare out over the black water to the horizon. I used to love looking across the ocean. It felt so vast, so infinite. A beautiful blank canvas. For me, it was my proof of a world beyond. A future filled with potential. Tonight, the moon shimmers on the water, and submarine lights twinkle faintly in the distance.

There are tears in my head, but nothing comes to the surface. I feel as if I'm in a trance. Tears feel useless. Then a splash. A small noise that interrupts the rhythm of wavelets against the hull. I hear it again, a splash like a fish breaking the surface.

I stand to look over the side of the boat where a dim glow moves in the water beneath me. It grows bigger and streaks away. In a burst, an enormous luminous fish leaps in the distance. Then I see. It's not a fish. It's him. It's *it*. Moving just beneath the surface toward the boat.

Suddenly, a head pops from the black water below me. I stumble back against the deck, but he stays there, just looking at me with round black eyes. He's beautiful. His face is shaped like a human's. An iridescent blue-green face with black feathery hair that falls to his shoulders like a man's.

He dives under quickly, and I can't see him. He is dark, no longer glowing, but the strokes of his tail light up trails of bioluminescent plankton in the water. He is swimming toward the back of the boat, and I follow.

At the swim platform, I step down to within inches of the water. So close, I could fall in. He comes up right next to me, and I jump away from the edge. His mouth is closed, but he looks like he is smiling. Small slits run along the sides of his nose, which is not really a nose so much as a narrow lavender-blue ridge.

He is studying my face, too, as if he is as curious about me as I am about him. As if he is thinking about it, analyzing it.

"Tss O'o ck ee."

Holy crap, it makes a noise.

"Tss O ck ee." Again. He lifts his hand out of the water. Five long silver-blue fingers reach into the air with his palm toward me. It shimmers, smooth and white like the belly of a dolphin. He stretches his arm, reaching his hand closer to the platform. I think he wants me to touch him. He's doing it again, "Ts Ock. . .Ts O' ckee."

It's a choppy kind of guttural sound. He's forcing air out in short bursts, but it sounds as if he's trying to say something. "Ts O'o Kee…Ts O Kee."

It sounds so much like "It's OK." His hand stretches toward me. He does want me to touch him. This is not believable. What should I do? I want to touch him. I want to talk to him. "It's OK," I say back to him and the corners of his mouth curl upward. "It's OK."

I reach my hand toward him and he turns his palm upward. His long fingers are closed together, cupped as if he's

98

holding water. My finger tips just barely touch the silky tips of his hands. A marine man! Maybe a siren! Barru Pi's mutant guards! I jump and stagger away from him, landing hard on my butt with my back against the steps. He flips into the water so fast he is gone before my eyes can follow.

Are the legends true? Did he want to lure me in? He didn't look like a guard, or a killer. This can't be real. I feel his fingertips still. Smooth. Firm. Were they warm? I don't know. Did he try to grab me? It was all so fast, I'm not sure what just happened. I think I scared him. I think we scared each other. But one thing I know, he spoke to me.

He spoke to me.

I sit there for hours. My knees tucked up against my chest, arms around my legs, my back pressed into the first step of the swim platform. I sit there watching the shimmering black water until the stars sink into the distant ocean and the sun rises.

*

I go through the motions of the day as if I were in a dream. Nothing is the same. There is a person in the water, living, thinking, talking. This is no mistake. I can't explain this away like I have been trying to do. This is real. Where is he now? What does he do all day? Is he swimming down there, watching us? What is he?

I can't tell anyone about this. They would think I'm crazy. I think I'm crazy. I have no idea what to do with this information. This is bigger than the Fouling.

All I want is for night to come, and for him to return. Right after dinner, I go to the bow with a light blanket to wait. Jake startles me from behind. "Mind if I sit up here with you?" he asks.

"Why not," I say. "It's your boat." We haven't spoken

much in the last five days. Not since I threw up, and Jake blasted me in my cabin for causing trouble. I help him with chores around the boat sometimes, but only as an excuse to avoid Dirk. We don't talk, just work.

He sits down next to me cross-legged. "I'm sorry I've been so harsh," he says.

"OK." I'm not very good at apologies. Besides, part of me feels like this is the "first mate" Jake talking. Be nice to the clients and all that.

"Just OK?" he says. "Come on, I've helped you out twice now, covering for you when you were swimming and diving where you shouldn't be."

"OK, then, thanks for that." I didn't ask him to do anything.

"There's a lot going on," he says. "To be honest, I wish I were in your shoes."

I know he does, and he probably deserves to be working on the science team as much as I do—maybe more. That's what makes me so annoyed at him. That and the fact that he lets the scientists misjudge him. He lets them think he's a high school dropout by choice.

"You've got this opportunity," he continues, "you're good at the science, and you're a good diver, so I can't understand why you keep pushing the limits."

This isn't the first mate Jake. It's the real Jake. He isn't mad at me, and he isn't being condescending. His blue eyes question me with genuine curiosity. He doesn't understand because I can't tell him.

"I'm sorry." There's not much more I can say. If I could, he would know that I'm not just blowing off this opportunity or being disrespectful. He would know I'm trying hard to keep it together. I'm trying to act normal while holding in this amazing, unbelievable, terrifying secret.

We sit side by side for a while, talking about the Fouling. He thinks it's odd that a thick, slimy algae covered the hull the day or two after we left Florida, and then again after we left the base on Cubbarros. Once he wipes it off, it doesn't return while we're out on the reef. The scientists say it's just algae we picked up in the harbor or in the shallows close to land. But Jake believes it's more than that. "I've been diving on my dad's boats my whole life," he says, "This stuff looks different."

"So, why don't you tell someone," I say.

"You heard what they said. What I think doesn't mean anything to them."

"Tell them again. Make them listen."

"Forget it, Alannis. I'm just a tour guide. I've probably been underwater more times than any of them, but they're the scientists."

"Jake, if you're sure it's something, you have to . . . ."

"I said forget it," he cuts me off, and there's no sense in pushing the subject. After a few awkward minutes of silence, Jake turns the focus on me. "Tell me about diving way up there in those cold, dark waters where you live." His voice is a little sarcastic.

"It's cold, it's dark, you can't see as much as you see here."

"That's it?" he asks.

"OK, well, what else do you want to know? When the visibility is bad, it's easy to get disoriented. You have to get used to working with your gear even when you can't see it. You use your hands a lot. When you go into a wreck, you have to bring a line so you can find your way back." It's hard to even think about diving back home right now, and he's putting me on the spot. "It's not like diving here for sure. Not as pretty and not as easy as diving in warm crystal clear water all the time."

Jake throws up a hand dismissively. "Oh, it's not so easy all the time," he laughs. "Out there, in blue water, you can't see the bottom. Talk about disorienting. There's nothing to tell you how deep you are when you're swimming around something like a whale or a pod of dolphin. One minute you're at 30 feet, and the next, you've drifted down to 60 because you're so set on watching them." It's as if he's been waiting to talk about this forever. "I got bumped once diving with a school of hammerheads out there. That's no joking around."

"What were you doing diving around hammerhead sharks?" I'm shocked. It's not something most people get to do. It's not something most people want to do.

"Do you think this is the only research team we've worked for?" he says. "Captain Sully runs a primo operation. Scientists, documentary filmmakers, rich divers with enough money to do all kinds of things they may not be qualified for. These guys use us all the time."

Jake has a ton of stories just waiting to spill out. It doesn't take much prodding to get him going. I can't believe all the things he's done. "Why haven't you said any of this before?" I ask him. "Any one of these stories would shut Dirk up in a heartbeat."

Jake laughs.

"I mean it," I say, "why don't you tell them how experienced you are?"

"No one ever asked me."

He is infuriating. What else is he keeping secret because no one ever asks?

I prod him to tell me more, but he says he's getting bored of his own voice. So, we talk about our families back home.

I'm missing the first buds emerging after winter, and I wish I could smell the spring air now. All the while, I'm looking out over the water for signs of my marine man. I hope he comes back. Soon. Maybe Jake will see. Eventually, fatigue overtakes me, and I lie on my back looking up into the sky. If he does return, I'll hear the splashing. Or Jake will see him. We talk quietly. His hushed voice begins to fade like background music.

When I wake, Jake is gone. A blanket covers me neatly, and my head rests on a boat cushion that wasn't there before. I spring to my feet and run to the side. Nothing but a white moon shining on the water. I wait. Listening, watching.

Then it happens. He returns.

He lifts his head and shoulders out of the water right under me and swims to the back of the boat. When he reaches his hand to me this time, he is too far away for me to touch him. "Come," he says. His voice is raspy, and hollow like a croaker fish. But it is clear. "Come," he says. "Come, Ts OK."

I may be crazy. This may be the stupidest thing I've ever done. The last thing I'll ever do. But I have to. "Ts OK."

I grab my mask and fins. I move to the end of the platform and swing my legs around, put them in the cool water. The marine man backs up, his hand still reaching toward me. OK, here goes. I put my mask on and slip into the water in my shorts and tank top. The full moon lights the first couple of feet beneath the surface. Beyond that, blackness. He has gone under about a foot and stays a couple of arms lengths away from me. I put my head underwater, and I hear him better than I see him. His voice comes in beats like a drum, but it is clearer underwater, and it is clearly English.

"Speak," he says, "can you speak?"

This is so not a dream. I'm weak with shock, with the

terror and the thrill of it all at the same time. I start to answer him underwater, forgetting I can't breathe here. I come to the surface coughing. He follows. I watch him watching me.

"Of course I can speak," I say. "How can you speak? Who are you?"

He sinks slowly underwater just to his forehead. When I put my head in, he says, "I'm Ra'Ook. I'm son to ShaOhm. I follo'd you from deh 'tsity." His words sound round and echoey like a drumbeat in the middle. But each syllable is clipped, as if he is swallowing them.

He raises his head above the surface and I pick my head up to speak. "Who is ShaOhm?" I ask. "What is *de 'tsity*?" As I say it, I realize he was saying "dead city." He followed us from the dead city. Does he mean the base? I let the air out of my lungs and pull myself down in the water. I need to hear his answer.

"ShaOhm. My father. Detsity. You swim by de 'tsity," he points up, "eighteen suns pass'd."

Eighteen suns. I calculate as quickly as I can. Was it only eighteen days ago when I first swam down the anchor line with Jake on my heels? Jake. I have to show someone. I have to get Jake.

I come to the surface and tell this marine man, this Ra'Ook, "Wait here. Can you wait? I need to get someone." He backs up in the water, but he stays while I get out. I put both hands up facing him. "Stay. Please stay here."

I run to the front of the boat and knock gently on Jake's door. There is no answer, but I don't want to wake anyone else. I'm afraid it'll scare Ra'Ook away. I run back to the platform, and he is still there waiting. As if I were a squirrel running back and forth across the road, I speed back to Jake's cabin door. Carefully, I turn the handle. Oh, man, I hope he wears clothes to bed.

"Jake," I whisper, jostling his shoulder a little bit. My wet hair drips on his neck as I reach over to see his face. "Wake up, Jake."

He rolls over, confused, and pulls his arm over his eyes. It takes a few agonizingly long seconds for him to realize it's me. "Come on," I beg him urgently. "I have to show you something. Now. Hurry, we have to go now."

"You're crazy," he whispers as I pull him toward the back of the boat, holding his hand in a death grip.

We get to the swim platform, and Ra'Ook is gone. There is nothing there. I feel sunken and defeated. I turn to Jake to explain, though I have no idea how to tell him. He is standing inches away from me, still holding my hand. He is a good four inches taller than I am. As he looks down at me, he chuckles quietly and says, "This is nice, I don't understand it, but—"

"Wait," I say, out of breath and near panic, "sit here with me. Just wait, you'll see." Where is Ra'Ook? We sit on the swim platform with our feet dangling in the water. My wet mask and fins lie scattered on the deck behind me. Jake hasn't seen them, thank goodness. He skootches closer to me and leans back on his hands. Come on, Ra'Ook. Where are you? Jake's shoulder presses against mine. He watches my face as I survey the water.

"So, what did you want to show me?" he teases, leaning in closer. When I turn, he is smiling at me, his eyebrows lifted high in question. My heartbeat hasn't stopped racing since I got in the water. Jake is so close, and he is real. All of this is real. If this is real, Ra'Ook is real. The moon is lighting Jake's face as if he's on a movie set. Spending these days with him has made me forget how good looking he is. He smiles curiously and I'm just so overwhelmed by everything that I laugh out loud and throw my arms around his neck. Inside I'm screaming, 'I saw a Ra'Ook. I talked with a Ra'Ook, and it was amazing.' But all Jake hears is my laughter. He pulls my arms away from his neck and says, "Shhh. What's up? Why now? I thought there might be something—"

"There *is* something," I say.

"but this is kind of sudden."

"That's just it," I tell him, "it's not sudden, I've known for days." Jake looks puzzled. I'm so excited to finally show someone the secret. Then it happens. A light beneath the water.

"Look." I point to it swimming below us. Jake pulls his legs out of the water and tries to pull me with him. I stand and yank my arm away. I leap to the deck, grab my mask and one for Jake. He's about to follow me up the steps when I push past him and dive into the water. Frantically, Jake dives in. He is on me in a second, trying to pull me back to the boat.

"Wait," I say. "Trust me." And I think of something that might make him stay. "It's just a whale, I saw it. Just stay a second."

Jake looks uneasy, but he takes the mask from me and puts it on. We dip our heads below the surface. Ra'Ook is swimming just beneath our feet. The sleek sides of his tail light the water, and I can barely make out his shape. Jake's entire body contracts in a spasm next to me. Then he's flailing his way back to the boat and pulling my arm along with him.

"What the hell was that?" Jake freaks out. "Oh shit, oh shit." He's alternating between trying to grab the side of the smooth hull, flailing his arms and legs, and putting his head back in the water to see.

Ra'Ook approaches us slowly and lifts his head out of the water just out of reach. Jake hoists himself onto the platform.

His hand has such a tight grip on my arm, I think he'll pull it out of its socket. I try to calm him, tell him it's alright. Ra'Ook smiles. He looks amused, but he doesn't leave.

Good, I think, *stay*. Stay and talk with us.

But Jake is out of control. I let him pull me out of the water. The shock, the fear in his eyes. His whole body on fire with survival instinct. I know this feeling. The world is a different place for him now, and it can never go back to the way it was.

I turn to Ra'Ook, but he is gone. Jake nearly collapses on the top step of the swim platform. I sit next to him and put my arm over his shoulder. He holds his arms tightly around himself and whispers, "Oh shit, oh shit, oh shit."

I take the first deep breath I've had in weeks. I am no longer alone.

CHAPTER 13

AFTER A WHILE, JAKE SITS UP STRAIGHT. "WE HAVE TO leave," he says. "We have to get out of here." He climbs to the back deck and puts his mask away, exactly where it belongs. He takes my wet fins that lie strewn on the deck and puts them away neatly. "What did that thing want?" he says, reaching for my mask. He puts it away without realizing what he's doing. "We have to go."

Jake is on auto-pilot. He runs toward the wheelhouse, but I stop him at the stairs. I put both hands on his shoulders and make him look at me. "Jake, stop. He's not hurting us. It's fine. I saw him that day. That's why I got sick. That's what scared me."

He's starting to register my voice. "What? You saw him before? Why didn't you tell anyone? Why didn't you tell me?"

"I was scared, and who would have believed me? I kept trying to convince myself it wasn't real. I was scared."

He looks right through me as if I'm not there. Something snaps him back to me. "Ha," he laughs like a crazy person. It borders on scary.

"Alannis, we have to tell someone," he says. "This is an amazing discovery; we just found something nobody will believe."

"I found it," I remind him. "This is my discovery." It feels childish even as I say it. "We don't know what he is or who

108

else knows about him, but we can't trust anyone here. We can't tell anyone until we find out more." I am emboldened by the fact that I'm no longer alone with the secret.

"Maybe we could catch one, bring it back," Jake says. He is a manic mess.

"We can't catch one," I tell him. "He's not fish or anything. His name is Ra'Ook."

"He has a NAME?"

"He talks, Jake. He told me he saw us over the wreck. He called it the dead city. His father is ShaOhm."

Jake is shivering. I have goose bumps from the cool breeze against my wet skin, but Jake is not cold, he is scared. "Come, on," I say, "we'll think about it in the morning." I take Jake's hand and lead him to his cabin. He lies down on his bunk and curls up facing the wall. I remember that night in my cabin when all I wanted from Sully was a hug. I wanted something to make me feel solid and safe. Without a word, I curl up in the bed against Jake's back and put my arms around him. He doesn't move, or say anything, but he presses my hand against his chest. I hold him until he falls asleep. It is nearly morning when I go back to my cabin and crawl into my bunk exhausted.

*

Jake is out of sorts and has been all day. He startles when someone calls his name. He told Sully he didn't want to go on their morning dive, and when he went in at noon to check the bottom, he put his regulator in his mouth upside down. I think Guillermo may know something. When he walked by us in the salon earlier, he put his hands on our shoulders and looked us each in the eyes. Then he nodded at Jake.

Exhausted from two nights without sleep, I go to bed early. I peek into Jake's room first.

"Meet me on deck at around two in the morning," I whisper.

He raises eyebrows. Then he squeezes his eyes shut and shakes his head. He's not ready to deal with this.

"Jake, look at me."

He won't open his eyes, but he sucks a breath in through his nose and says "I'll be there."

Like clockwork, the moon wakes me, streaming through the porthole. I whisper Lacey's name to make sure she is asleep. When she doesn't answer, I slide down and reach my foot across to the vanity. My bunk ladder creaks, so I have to clamber down the other side of the cabin to keep from disturbing her.

I'm about to tiptoe out the cabin door when Lacey says, "Don't do something stupid."

My heart leaps. "What?"

"I don't want to sound like a mom, but you're only sixteen," she says. "He's sweet, but just be careful. You don't need to rush into anything."

Oh no, she thinks I'm getting up to be with Jake and I'm horrified. "But, I'm not, we're not—"

She cuts me off. "I know, the diving, the water, the beauty of it all. It distorts things." Oh my god, will she just shut up! "Be smart about it. You have your whole life for romance."

I rush out of the cabin without saying anything in response. Jake is on deck when I get there.

"What took you so long?" he says, offering me half of the blanket wrapped around his shoulders. I ignore the offer and sit across from him. Lacey's words ring in my ears, which have grown hot and are probably as red as tomatoes. I'm sure my whole face is red. "What, we're not friends now?" Jake says.

"Listen," I tell him, "my roommate thinks I've been out

all night with you for the past two nights. She's not a very quiet person, so it's a pretty sure thing everyone else thinks the same thing about me."

Jake smirks and wraps the blanket around himself. "Why do you care so much what other people think?"

"What other people think doesn't bother me personally, but it does affect how they treat me. You should think a little more about that yourself."

"Well, I don't let other people's opinions get to me," he says, scooting a little closer with a sly grin on his face. "Besides, is it so bad if they think you and I have a little thing going on?"

"Yes, it is, Jake. This is about professionalism. I can't be seen with you like this." I regret my words as soon as they come out of my mouth. His grin drops instantly, and I hear how that sounded to him. As if a romantic relationship with a high school dropout and dive jockey will make me look bad. It's not what I meant, but it doesn't matter. He's given up on earning their respect, and I have just slapped him in the face with it.

Tension fills the space between us until suddenly, Ra'Ook porpoises across the bow. I run to the stern and grab my gear. Jake is right behind me, but as I sit down on the platform to slide in, he blocks my way with his arm. "Easy," he says. "You don't know for sure what this thing will do." When I slip in the water, Jake stops my hand on the platform. "Right here," he says. "You hold on, right here." Then he gets in beside me, gripping the edge of the platform.

Ra'Ook pops up in front of me. He's never been quite this close. The ridge on his face subtly changes color in the moonlight the way a soap bubble changes as it moves. He is so beautiful. It's hard to imagine him as some horrible lab experiment, or a trained animal of the Commission. If I put my hand up, I could touch his face. Ra'Ook submerges, swims a few feet away, and goes deeper. My instincts tell me this isn't a good idea, but I want to swim to him.

Jake moves closer and puts his arm in front of me. Having someone else here gives me more courage, as if somehow there is safety in numbers. With Jake holding me back, my natural response it to resist him. I want to go even more. Jake expects me to swim forward, but I sink straight down, and he doesn't have a chance to stop me.

I swim down about 15 feet, following the stream of glowing plankton behind Ra'Ook. He stops and his skin flashes with bright white light that quickly dissolves into a display of sunset colors, oranges and reds and peach. I've seen cuttlefish do this in an aquarium, but this is magnificent. Ra'Ook turns around to face me. Underwater, his black hair stands on end and sways like a field of grasses. Suddenly it flattens back down against his head and he shoots up to the surface. As I swim up, the moonlight pierces the slick water in rays. Ra'Ook has leapt completely out of the water, and plunged back down in a missile of bubbles.

"Did you see that?" I call to Jake. He is still holding on to the boat, waving me back.

Jakes eyes widen, and I turn to see Ra'Ook come up behind me. He is still. His deep eyes are soft. I feel completely safe with him now. He doesn't want to hurt us. He wants to know us. Jake swims to me, grabs my arm and tries to pull me toward the boat.

"Do all of your people speak English?" I say. Ra'Ook laughs with a dry, croaky voice.

Jake stops, looks at Ra'Ook and stutters, "What the. . ."

I tug Jake beneath the water with me to listen for Ra'Ook's answer. "No," Ra'Ook says. "I am son to am 'bass 'dor. I grew up ssspeak' ging' your words. ShaOhm teach'es me."

I am transfixed, and I don't even realize Jake has been dragging me back until he nearly pushes me against the bottom of the boat. He is gripping the platform again.

"Ambassador to what?" Jake asks.

Ra'Ook tries to say something above water. It sounds like "T' Eeyoo." But I can't understand him, so I pull Jake under and Ra'Ook follows us.

"To your people. I have not ss'een to one before," Ra'Ook says. He looks at Jake. "You are the male?"

Jake nods his head, yes.

"You are a pair?" Ra'Ook looks back and forth between us.

The question stuns me. Jake and I look at each other. We shake our heads no.

Over the course of a few minutes of bobbing up and down, Ra'Ook asks us if our people pair. If we spawn or are live-bearing. He asks how many years we each have and if we're siblings. The more I listen, the easier it is to understand him. I'm embarrassed by the questioning until it occurs to me that Ra'Ook is asking all the questions I should be asking him.

"How old are you?" I ask him.

"Eighteen years."

"Where do you come from?" I say.

"Here," he answers. That was not worded well. I have to be more specific.

"Do you have a family?" I ask.

"Yes."

Of course, he already said his father is ambassador. I can't think of a good question fast enough. Everything I wanted to know evaporates from my brain. This odd way of speaking above water, listening below.

"Are you here for war?" he asks us. "My father says you are here for the war."

Jake's head punches through the surface, interrupting Ra'Ook with its force. "What war?" he says. "There is no war."

Ra'Ook sinks down just low enough that his mouth and nose are underwater. His eyes fix on Jake.

"No war?" he says. "Hundreds of years your people and my people, we fight. We are afraid. It is only here we are safe. Until you come and want more."

"More what? We aren't here to take anything from you," I say.

"My father's father learned your words to end the fear. Fifty years now, we have your treaty. ShaOhm, remembers. He learned your words from his father. They are the talkers. You call them ambassadors, but you lie to them. You break this treaty and say this is not war?"

"You're crazy. This is crazy." Jake says flailing beside the boat with a death grip on my arm.

"Crazy?" Ra'Ook says. "Why have you come here to find us? Why? I am not so rigid as my father. When I am the talker, I will not use your words to speak war. I want to understand this." I can see a dim flashing beneath Ra'Ook's skin. Like flames behind smoky glass.

"We don't mean any harm to you," I say. "We did not come to find you."

"Our people are not at war with you," Jake says, kicking himself onto the platform with me still in his grip. "Get out Alannis. We have to get out."

"Come back," I call to Ra'Ook. "Come back again." He watches Jake haul me onto the platform. Jake grips my arm so tightly, I'm afraid it will leave another bruise like the one he gave me last night. I had to wear a long sleeve rash guard all day so no one would see it.

On the platform I'm beside myself.

"War!" Jake says. "What does that thing mean, war? What does it want?"

"If you hadn't pulled us out of the water, and been so aggressive, maybe we would know," I growl.

"If it's looking for war, we should shoot the thing if it comes back."

Jake surprises me. I can only assume he is talking out of fear. "It's not a thing," I say. "It is a he. A HE Jake. A new species." I feel the weight of the words as I say them. "He's a totally new species."

Jake takes a few deep breaths and slows himself down. He grabs on to both of my arms. "I don't know what that was, but it's not right." He isn't even trying to keep his voice down. "All that, 'Do you pair? Do you spawn?' It thinks we're animals or something. And it definitely doesn't see people as friends."

I take a moment for the first time to think about what this discovery really means. I imagine what it must have been like for ancient explorers to discover something so like them, say a chimp or a gorilla. What would they have thought? But Ra'Ook is not a gorilla. He speaks. He thinks like we do. He is almost human. This would change humanity. It would turn our world view upside-down. I could study him, find out where he lives, what kind of home he has. Does he have his own language? Do his people have a culture? I would be the first marine anthropologist. I would become an icon in the scientific world. Bigger than Darwin.

"This is not real," Jake argues. "It's some kind of freak accident. Some mutant caught in Barru Pi's toxic attack on her own people." He is pacing back and forth.

115

"No," I argue, "didn't you hear him? Ra'Ook said we've been fighting for hundreds of years." In my mind, I replay everything Ra'Ook told us. They were safe here until we came. The treaty. Fifty years. That's how long the Commission has been in charge. "Can't you see it? The Commission knows about them."

Jake shakes his head 'no' like he doesn't want to hear any more.

"Don't you get it?" I say. "The treaty is with the Commission."

It is beginning to sink in just how dangerous this is. As much as the powerful leaders around the world condemn the Commission, they do nothing to curb its power. They formed it, and yet they say they can't control it. Why?

"Jake," I urge him to look at me. "Think about it, why would the Commission start taking over the ocean once Barru Pi was gone? Why do they sink ships and intimidate the world? It doesn't make sense. There is no reason to control the oceans unless. . ." I almost don't want to say what I'm thinking. As if the words will make it true. "Unless their real purpose is to keep Ra'Ook and his people hidden, to keep all of this a secret." How deep does this secret go?

Jake is silent. He puts his goggles and fins away. Wordlessly, he dries himself off and hangs his towel neatly over the rail before folding the blanket and marching to his cabin. I know this kind of anger. It is the anger my brother shows when he is scared.

*

I wake to the sound of the anchor, and run up to the deck. Did Jake tell Sully? Is that why we're leaving? Guillermo stops me at the door to the main salon.

"We are in rush this morning, yes?" he inquires.

"Why are we leaving? Where are we going?" I ask him as I realize Matt and Candace are sitting around the settee having breakfast.

"We're going to the base," Candace says.

"Resupply time," Matt adds, holding up the last mango.

CHAPTER 14

ON THE WAY TO THE BASE, I CORNER JAKE IN THE WHEEL-house. I've been trying to get him alone all morning, but he's been careful to stay within earshot of the others. When I close the door behind me, he looks like he's about to say something until I cut him off. Sully might come up here any minute, and Jake has to know everything before we get to the base.

"Listen to me. That first day, the day we went swimming in the black out zone and saw that wreck—"

"We don't know that's what it was," he interrupts.

"Whatever Jake, I'm trying to tell you, last time we were at the base, I went with one of the guards to get water, and they sat me down and interrogated me."

"Because of the wreck?" he asks. I don't tell him that he just admitted it was a wreck.

"Maybe. They kept asking me if I saw something that scared me. Maybe it's not about the wreck specifically. I think maybe we were the ones who broke the treaty when we swam down there. This is their water, Jake. Ra'Ook's water. What if we broke the treaty just by being there? Now, his father thinks we're here to make war."

He opens his mouth to speak, but I'm not letting him get a word in until I've finished.

"There's more. After Dirk caught us swimming, I heard him talking with Guillermo. And Guillermo said the

Commission would track us down and kill us. They're mad, Jake."

Jake shakes his head. "I can't believe this. This is so screwed up."

"This is about more than just me, or us. Guillermo also thinks the Cubbarros islands will be blamed for the Fouling."

"That's crazy," Jake argues, "Barru Pi is dead."

"Yes, she's dead, but if people think the Fouling comes from here, if they think it's one of her experiments that's spreading, Guillermo may be right. People might want to destroy the islands just to get rid of it. He thinks the Navy submarines will blow the reef to pieces when we leave."

Jake shakes his head. "Sounds like your fishboy is going to get his war. Even if it isn't the same one he's thinking about."

"Jake, I can't go back to the base. If they interrogate me again, I don't think my lies will convince them. They'll know I've seen Ra'Ook."

"You stay with me when my father pulls into the dock," he says. "You're not going ashore in the morning, no matter what."

As we approach the dock, Jake works the port side of the boat and the bow; I work the stern, securing ropes to the cleats on deck. When we're close enough, Jake steps off the boat. I hand him the lines, which he loops in clove hitches around each piling. He steps back aboard, and we scurry below while Sully meets with the Commission officer.

In the morning, the Commission says nothing about letting the team go ashore. Matt and Sully will be the only ones to collect our supplies. Guillermo refuses to go ashore again. He said their pavement and stucco buildings destroyed the beauty of his home, and it's no longer his island. I stay in the wheelhouse crouched low in the copilot's seat with a book, although trying to read is useless. I should be working on that school report but it seems so insignificant right now. Instead, I peer over the console to watch what's going on. Jake waits on deck for a uniformed dock guard to bring him a water line. He fills the water tanks, and empties the holding tanks and trash. Dirk and Lacey hang around the guards again. What will Dirk tell them this time?

Matt and Sully finally come walking down the dock with a cart full of food and toilet paper. We have our supplies, and it takes just a half an hour before we're ready to shove off.

Once we're away from the island, Dirk asks everyone to join him on the upper deck. Sully listens to the conversation from the doorway of the wheelhouse. Dirk and Lacey relay the latest news on the Fouling, and it's horrifying. Impossibly, the Fouling has spread 300 miles in the last week. There is nothing else in nature that is this aggressive. It is now in Delaware. In addition, eight more ships have been lost in the North Atlantic. Cold waters. There's still no sign of the Fouling in Europe or Africa yet, but in all likelihood, ships have already carried it there. It's just a matter of time. To be safe, the European and African shipping trades have completely stopped with the hope they can prevent it from spreading into the Indian Ocean. Already, in Central America, the Fouling has almost reached the Panama Canal. If it gets through, it will take over the Pacific in no time.

The riots are increasing, and there is a curfew now across most countries in North and South America. Even with the curfew, people are camping out on the streets in front of the White House with signs demanding the government do something. There isn't much they can do if they can't stop the Fouling. The guards told Dirk and Lacey what they knew, but there is no word from home. Nothing about what's going on in Braverton Bay or at the university. We are mostly silent for the rest of the day. Even Matt has nothing to say.

The sun has just dipped below the horizon when we arrive onsite. Most of us are on the top deck brooding about the urgency of this expedition. Our goal may be impossible at this point. We're desperate to succeed. As the sky darkens, a distinct cluster of lights appears in the distance. The submarines are still there. Waiting for an order, I suspect. It's grossly ironic, but if we can't find a solution to the Fouling here, the one place in the world that isn't affected by it will be destroyed.

At dinner, the scientists talk about changing dive sites again. Perhaps both varieties of Fouling are here on the reef and we just haven't found *the Fouling* yet. Then Jake gets up and leaves the table quickly without saying anything. A few minutes later. Jake just jumps into the dark water. He doesn't even have any scuba gear, just a mask and fins. Within a few minutes he climbs back onboard and walks up to us dripping wet with a green scrubby pad in his hand. It's covered in a thick slime that looks like algae.

"You have to consider this," he says firmly. "This is something. I'm positive."

Dirk pushes out his bottom lip and shrugs his shoulders. He's not impressed, but Jake continues. "This stuff is thicker and stickier than anything I've ever cleaned off of the bottom of a boat before. It only shows up after we've been in water where the Fouling exists. It was there the day after we left home, and it's been there each time we came back from the base. I scrub it off, and as long as we're out here, it doesn't come back." Jake pushes the slimy muck toward each of the scientists as he speaks.

Matt reaches across the table, takes the scrubby and examines it. "I'll take a look under the scopes," he says while it drips seawater all over the table next to his plate. "You never know." I do a little cheer in my head. 'YES! Finally, Jake speaks up.'

In the galley I help him do the dinner dishes. The whole team is in the salon, so we can't speak freely, but he leans over close to me and whispers in my ear, "We can't go back in the water with it."

Knowing how this must look to everyone else, him whispering in my ear, I pull away and look him in the eye. He can't mean that. We have to go back in. We have to learn everything we can about Ra'Ook. "Too risky," he mouths without a sound. When we're done washing, he leans over again. "You don't know what it might do. Or what someone else might do if they caught us talking to it." Then he walks out of the salon and heads forward to his cabin. I can't follow him without confirming everything they already think of me.

That evening, I lie in bed waiting for Lacey to go to sleep. She tosses beneath me for a long time, and I go back and forth thinking about what Jake said. Since we left the site, I have been afraid Ra'Ook will not come back when we return. Jake may have scared him away, or he may have gone when we left the site. I can't just lie here waiting to talk about this with Jake. If Ra'Ook is going to be out there tonight, I have to go.

Jake is already at the back of the boat when I get there. He is rigging two full-face masks. "I knew you wouldn't listen," he says. "This is a bad idea, but I'm not letting you do it alone." He holds one of the masks up to my face. "If you've never used one, it's easy. We use them to video some of our clients. They like to talk to the camera underwater."

With my chin wedged into the mask, he pulls the straps

up over my head and snugs them. "Do you have a good seal?" he asks. The clear glass mask covers my whole face. I can see all around me. Most importantly, with this mask, I don't have to hold a regulator in my mouth. I can speak underwater.

Jake tells me how to push my nose against a little pad inside the mask so I can clear my ears on descent. He raps the top of my head with his knuckles making a loud vibrating bang throughout my skull. "We're staying at the surface," he says sternly. "We're not going below three feet with fishboy."

I take the mask off and watch him go over every piece of equipment, silently double-checking every hose attachment and valve. This is risky. There is no way we could explain this if someone were to come out and see us right now. I wonder if it would have been better to stick to the simple mask and mouthpiece regulator.

I sit on the platform and kick my fins lightly in the water. *Please, hear me Ra'Ook. Please come back.* Then the faint glimmer of bioluminescence outlines his wake. He doesn't come up, so Jake and I slip in and look below us. A light goes on like a bulb. Ra'Ook has pushed what looks like a jellyfish over his head. It pulses above him, illuminating the water with a white-green glow.

I sink into the dark water. My hand stretches overhead to keep contact with the underside of the boat. Ra'Ook stays where he is. Maybe it's Jake's presence, but he won't come closer, so I let go of the boat and swim a few feet toward him. Jake follows and Ra'Ook's skin rapidly shifts from blue and green to purple and then orange.

"No," I say holding Jake back. "I need to go alone. He was not the same when you were there. Your tension, I think it scares him."

"No kidding. He kind of scares me, too," Jake snaps back.

"He trusts me," I say. "He chose me."

As I swim away from Jake, the light dims and Ra'Ook dives into the blackness. I am suspended in the dark water with no vision of what lies just outside my reach. The sound of Jake's breathing reaches me in tumbling bubbles and mechanical whooshes. I float in a void, but I know I am not alone. Whatever is out there can see me, smell me, feel me. This is probably a good time to head back to the boat. Then, suddenly Ra'Ook is right in front of me.

I'm ready with my questions. I want to know who his father is dealing with. What does he know about the Commission? Who does he think broke the treaty? Does Ra'Ook live in the blackout zones? How many others like him are there?

With the full-face mask, I have a clearer view of everything around me. It's like looking through a window instead of a tunnel, which is what my regular dive mask is like. I breathe freely, and move my jaw around to form my first words.

"Rook," I say to him.

The corners of his mouth stretch up into a closed smile, and his eyes scrunch with amusement. "Ra'Ook," he says back, chopping his name into two sharp parts. It sounds much different than my attempt.

"Alannis," I say, pointing to my chest.

"Al' Ans," he repeats. He looks at my hands sculling the water beside me, reaches for the right one, holds it up in front of our faces. His fingers slide down my palm to my forearm. His hands are nearly twice as long as mine. The back side of his hands and arms are that same shimmery blue green. His palms are silvery grey and white. They are soft like skin covered in silky baby powder. "What's it like?" he says.

"Land?"

I watch him turn my hand over, open my fingers one at a time. "Dry," I stutter. "Land is dry." I am lost with no words.

Ra'Ook looks at my legs and sinks gently down to wrap his hand around my knee, feeling it bend and straighten as I kick slowly to keep myself stable in the water. He is not exactly warm, but his hands are not cool like the water. I can't believe what I'm doing.

Ra'Ook inspects my legs like a child seeing something for the first time. He slides his hands toward my feet. I reach down and slip off one of my fins. His head jerks back quickly. His surprised eyes dart up to my face. I laugh inside the mask, and bubbles billow out. He takes my foot in both hands. It feels so weirdly personal, so intimate. It's just my foot, but I don't think anyone has ever touched my feet like this before. He inspects my toes. When he slips a finger between two of them, it tickles and I jerk my foot away. I reach down to put my fin back on, bending awkwardly in the water.

While he watches me, I realize how big he is. If his tail were two legs with feet instead of fins, he would probably be seven feet tall. I swim close to him and bring my hand to his face. Seven narrow slits run up each side of the gentle ridge that looks like a nose. As they open and close, two long folds along the sides of his face pulse lightly. Gills, maybe. His forehead is rounder at the top than a person's. High above his eyes, above a ridge where eyebrows should be, there are two deep folds. They're shaped like eyebrows, but they're more like blowholes. He is so human-like, and still so incredibly different.

He puts his hands up, and I reach for them, turn them over. Studying them the way he inspected mine. We float vertically a few feet below the surface. We hold our hands up to face one another, touch our palms together. The underside of the water glistens in the moon like a mirror above us.

I run my fingertips down the shimmery skin of his forearm. It feels thick, no hair. He opens his palm and spreads his fingers. Veins run through the translucent web of skin that connects them. I lace my fingers between his and gently move them down to feel the webs. I expect them to resist, but they give way easily. As they retract, the skin pulls away from his finger tips unveiling black dagger-like claws.

I pull away in shock. Ra'Ook startles. "Do I scare you?" he asks. I push down the fear—partly because I don't want to hurt his feelings, but mostly, it's instinct. The warning voice in my head tells me to never show fear to a predator.

"No," I croak, "I just didn't know."

I hear a slapping sound and know that Jake is urging me back to the boat. I had forgotten about Jake. When I come on deck, he says, "What the hell was all that? You let him touch you? He could have killed you."

"He didn't," I hear myself say. It's as if I'm not really here, I'm floating above the boat, watching us. The only sensation I'm aware of right now is Ra'Ook's fingertips on my feet. A gentle, lingering pressure.

"Well, what did you find out, what did he say?"

I look at him blankly. How do I describe that?

CHAPTER 15

I CAN'T BEGIN TO TELL JAKE WHAT JUST HAPPENED. I CAN'T even process it myself yet. Jake has taken off his mask and is loosening the straps to mine while I stand here, helpless. "It was amazing," is all I manage to say.

We put away our gear carefully, making sure our used tanks are in the back row with the spares. The work brings me down to Earth a little. I tell Jake that Ra'Ook touched my feet, and that his hands were silky, his face a remarkable array of colors. Jake is impatient, grilling me for answers to questions I never asked. Tomorrow night, I promise him. Tomorrow we'll find out everything.

*

The next morning, I wake up counting the seconds until night falls. Dirk is by my side all day as we dive, watching every move I make. I know Ra'Ook won't come, but I look for him anyway. After dinner, I tell Lacey I want to take my place at the compressor again. I don't relish the idea of filling tanks with Dirk, but I have to make sure the spare tanks are refilled. I just have to figure out how to do it without Dirk noticing. As I expected, Lacey joins us. Her chatter and his obsession with his own stories provide the perfect diversion.

Again, Jake meets me on deck at night and we both go in the water. He waits next to the boat while I meet Ra'Ook just a few yards away. I ask him who his father works with as an ambassador. Who does he have a treaty with? I don't think he understands my question. He tells me his father expects him to become ambassador some day, but he wants to learn more about land and its people first. His answers frustrate me.

"Who broke the treaty?" I ask.

"This is not my war," he answers. "I hope to choose a different path."

"But who are you at war with, and what did they do?"

He looks at me with narrowed eyes. "You send us the black death, and you ask this? You say this is not war?"

It's crazy if Ra'Ook thinks we brought the Fouling here. "We did not send the black death," I explain. "We are trying to stop it."

He floats straight up and down, so still in the water, just his tail moving smoothly back and forth. He says nothing, just looks at me as if he's studying my face. I feel bulky and clumsy, with my heavy gear and loud breathing. It seems stupid to say we're trying to stop this thing in his world. . .as if we have that kind of control. We're so out of place here, we know so little about his world.

"What's it like," I ask, "to move through the water like that?" He circles me effortlessly then dives down with two elegant strokes of his tail. His wake glows beneath me, and he zooms back up behind me and taps me on the shoulder. His eyes are laughing, his head shaking back and forth. He curls his lips into a smile that reveals a row of sharp, jagged teeth.

Ra'Ook swims an arm's length away from me and says, "Come." How much clearer this sounds than the first time I heard him speak. It's the same with Guillermo's rich, lyrical accent which has become easy to understand as I've grown used to it. At the boat, a white stream of bubbles rises from Jake's silhouette. Ra'Ook reaches his hand toward me, and I take it. He pulls me closer to him and my whole body stiffens. Warily, I let him guide my arms over his shoulders. He brings my hands behind his neck and gives them a firm squeeze so I will grip them together. Then he takes off. It's like being strapped to a torpedo. Water streams by us so quickly, I have to press my face into his chest to keep my mask from being whisked away. My eyes squeeze shut out of reflex. I tell myself not to hold my breath, and it comes out in short heavy bursts, like panting.

We're traveling so fast. We've gone too far from the boat. What if he won't go back? I close my arms tighter around Ra'Ook's neck. I have trusted him to keep me safe, but this feels anything but safe. Where is he taking me? Perhaps this was a bad idea. Trust and fear battle each other in my tightened chest as we flash through the water. I feel my body shifting into survival mode. Quickly, I weigh my options:

Push away from him and tumble through the water with my mask ripped from my face at torpedo speed.

Scream for him to stop and reveal my terror and my weakness.

Hold on and hope he will bring me back safely.

While the alarms grow louder in my head, Ra'Ook suddenly launches us into the air. I gasp and squeeze him in a death grip. My stomach drops as if I were cresting a roller coaster and we plunge back down in a violent explosion of bubbles. Before I have time to brace for whatever is coming next, he has brought me back to the boat. It's over. Relief, excitement, lingering fear, all swirl together and pour out of me in gasps. He lets go of me and holds his two hands up. I hold mine up to them. Our fingertips barely touch.

"Until tomorrow's moon," he says.

Jake is frantic in the water beside me. His hands grapple

for my shoulders, grabbing the valve on the top of my tank as if to drag me in a rescue maneuver. "I'm fine," I shriek, kicking away. "Let me go. I can swim."

Out of the water, we sit on deck with our gear still on. Jake's mouth hangs open, his wide eyes pressing me to speak.

My legs and arms tremble. "I asked him what it felt like to swim like that."

He leans back on his hands. "Are you sick? This is so wrong. That thing almost killed you."

Jake is right, but only partly. Ra'Ook COULD have killed me. He didn't. "He won't hurt me," I say.

Jake wipes wet curls away from my face. "Look at you," he says. "You're not thinking right. You're in over your head." I brush his hand away. It feels rough and small, but I don't resist as he unbuckles my BC and removes my tank. My legs feel like Jello. When he has my gear put away, Jake wraps a towel around me, leaving his arm over my shoulder. I collapse into him and close my eyes. I still feel the power of shooting through the water with Ra'Ook.

"Ra'Ook said we sent the black death," I tell him wearily. "He blames us the way the rest of the world will blame Barru Pi. He thinks the Fouling is a weapon against them."

"Well, if it is a weapon, it isn't a very effective one," Jake sneers. "This is the only place it isn't working."

Suddenly the dots connect. We look at each other and say at once, "They know how to stop it."

CHAPTER 16

LAST NIGHT WAS THE MOST AMAZING EXPERIENCE OF MY life. I've thought of nothing else all day. Whether I was diving, or cleaning gear, or eating, or talking with someone, concentrating on anything has been like trying to recite the declaration of independence with heavy metal blaring in my ears. Seeing Ra'Ook tonight is the only thing on my mind. I have to focus this time. There is so much at stake. I'm ready to find out everything I can.

Jake and I meet on deck at two in the morning. He sets up our gear while I watch for signs that someone else might be up. The cabins are far forward, and we're being very quiet, but I'm still worried we'll be caught out here with all our dive gear and no good explanation. Jake has emptied one of the gear lockers beneath our feet so we'll have a place to ditch the gear quickly if we hear someone moving around on deck. Hopefully it will be quick enough.

The submarines are so far away, their lights so dim in the distance; it's hard to distinguish them from the sparkling moonlight on the water. If I didn't know to look for them, I might not even know they were there. Surely they can't see us, but we're sitting on something so unbelievable, just being out here feels risky.

I've asked Jake to show me how to recover and clear a full face mask underwater. Clearing a normal mask or recovering a regulator that gets knocked away from me is easy, something every diver practices. But a full face mask is more intimidating.

"No way. You're not leaving my side this time," he argues, "and you won't be diving down at all."

"Never mind that. I don't feel safe without proper training."

Reluctantly he agrees to show me what to do, and we slip into the water to practice. He's taught dozens of divers how to do this, and his confidence is comforting.

When Ra'Ook appears away from the boat, I put my hands up and signal for him to come closer. Jake has agreed to try to be more open minded, to trust Ra'Ook and act a little more friendly. He will start off with some simple questions. Nothing about war or the black death. The first thing Jake asks him is, "How many of you are there?"

He tells us his whole family lives here. He says this is their water, and that there are thousands of them. Jake and I move a little closer to one another at the thought of thousands of Ra'Ooks swimming all around us in the dark.

"Where are they?" I ask. "Where does everyone live?"

"In our homes," he says. "I can show you."

"Yes," I answer for both of us in a rush of curiosity. "Yes, we want to see. Can you take us there?" Jake grabs my forearm, and I realize I probably should have thought about it first.

"Only one," Ra'Ook says. "It is far. We will be gone until the light comes." Jake shakes his head *no*. "I will show you what you want to know," Ra'Ook adds. That's it, I'm going. I have to trust him. He brought me back last night. He could have taken me anywhere, thrown me around the way a killer whale plays with a seal before killing it. But he didn't.

"I'm going. That's it." I take one kick to the surface. Jake and Ra'Ook follow me, and I take a quick glance at Jake. His wide eyes fill with concern.

"Alannis, no. This is too dangerous. If you leave, I'll get my father. I'll get Dirk," he threatens. He knows by the time he wakes someone, I will be gone. He can't stop me. When he throws his arms around me, our clunky gear smashes together in an uncomfortable tangle that pushes me below the water. We separate, and Jake holds both of my hands tightly against his chest.

"Don't do this," he pleads.

"I have to. I'll be fine," I promise. "Wait for me."

As we speed through the water, Ra'Ook lifts me once into the air. The *Sun Joule*, my life support system bobs farther and farther away in a vast black ocean. After what feels like an hour underwater, I have to squeeze Ra'Ook's neck hard to get him to stop. I need a break. I need to rest and look around me, take off my mask, breathe real air from the sky.

Above the water, tall island peaks blacken the sky in front of us. Waves crash thunderously against the shore. The warm night air on my face feels refreshing, and I wonder how far we've come. There are no submarines on the horizon. Are we close to his home? Will there be a family of underwater people like him. Will they be sleeping, or are they nocturnal? Do they snatch fish with their hands and eat them, or do they dig for clams and crabs? Do they sleep with one eye open like dolphins? I can't even begin to imagine what their homes look like. Where could they possibly live?

Maybe I will meet his father, the ambassador. I could explain about the Fouling, ask if he can help us stop it. After about ten minutes, I'm ready to go again. Ra'Ook waits with his hand around my waist while I clear my mask. Suddenly he darts away. I sweep my arms across the surface of the water, spinning myself around to look for him in all directions. When I put my face in, a faint glow streaks beneath me.

Something big and solid slams into me from behind. I'm knocked forward, and I struggle to reorient myself. When I lift my head out of the water, I see a dark triangular shape barreling toward me. The unmistakable fin of a shark. Time slows down, and everything seems to happen in slow motion. It's pushing a wake of white foam in front of it like the bow of a small boat. Where is Ra'Ook? The shark is close. Moving fast. No time for thoughts. Inches. It's going to happen.

Time snaps back when something hits the water so hard, I feel the percussion. A blur of black mass and energy explodes, and I try to swim away from it. As if the island suddenly appeared in front of me, a huge dark mountain rises up out of the water. A gaping mouth. Gnashing teeth. I close my eyes against a sudden painful death. My scream echoes in my facemask.

The sound of a tree falling. My eyes open just in time to see the shark lifted into the air. Ra'Ook's shoulder plows the beast up and away from me. They plunge back into the water. Ten, maybe fifteen feet away, the water boils with their thrashing. Then they disappear. I bend my head down to see underwater. Ra'Ook is gone. The shark is barely visible as it circles around and begins to swim slowly back to me. Out of darkness, a streak of light speeds toward the shark from below. It's Ra'Ook, his arm stretched back as if he's winding up to punch the giant animal. He is inches from the shark's underbelly when he thrusts his forearm forward. A row of spikes hinges out from his elbow like the sail on the back of a swordfish, and Ra'Ook slashes the shark open. The claws of his other hand gouge into its gills, and he rips the animal through the water. A cloud of blood surrounds me.

Ra'Ook slams into me and we charge away at full speed with his arms around my waist—arms that feel strong and unforgiving. Arms with deadly spikes and claws hidden just beneath the skin.

By the time Ra'Ook stops, I am completely exhausted. We have been traveling for what seems like hours. "We are home," he says, but I see nothing but blackness. He takes my hand and dives. With his other hand stretched overhead, he lights the abyss in front of us. We follow the edge of a sharp cliff that teems with life. Night creatures swarm the jagged reef, transforming it into something alien to me. Lobster, crabs, thin white eels. Octopus skirt along the rocky corals. A parrot fish lies still, sleeping in a bubble of mucous, clear like jelly.

The pressure in my ears mounts with our increasing depth. Clearing them is unfamiliar in the full face mask, but I carefully repeat what I practiced with Jake. We continue our descent. Deeper. Deeper. I check my computer. 80 feet. We should really stop soon. I've never dived beyond 90 feet, but we quickly pass 90 and then 100. I'm dizzy with it. Dizzy with depth.

I say that again in my head. Dizzy with Depth. It sounds funny. I look at Ra'Ook, and laugh. I'm Drunkenly Dizzy with Depth. That's Fairly Funny.

And suddenly it's not. I'm not thinking clearly. The words nitrogen narcosis reach into my consciousness with a rush of fear—rapture of the deep. It can be dangerous. Clouded thoughts, confusion, bad decisions. Like a drunkard on a tight rope. This can be deadly if I don't get it together. Focus. Stay focused. Look at my computer. 160 feet. That's worrisome. I try to let go of Ra'Ook. I need to get to the surface. But he's got me. 170 feet, 180, 190. My heart pounds against my ears *ba-boom-boom, ba-boom-boom*. The drumbeat pushes all of the words out of my head. I can't think at all. We're getting close to a real danger zone. Past 200 feet, oxygen can be toxic. Divers convulse, lose consciousness. Die.

I'm nauseous, so dizzy. "Ra'Ook," I try to call out, "Ra'Ook."

CHAPTER 17

I DON'T KNOW IF I PASSED OUT FOR A SECOND, BUT I THINK we're swimming beside some sort of wall. Things flash and glow on that side as we pass by. Snapping, crackling sounds. Shrimp and crabs eating. Lights darting in front of us in the dark. Ra'Ook is pulling me into the wall. Everything goes black.

We're in some kind of tunnel, now. Ra'Ook's swimming me up. Little lights surround us. Little sparkling fingers sweeping over us as we rise through them. It's like a carwash full of glowing ribbons. Up, up. I'm aware of my breathing now. It slows, grows deeper, calmer. My head clears. We're not in a tunnel. We're in a cavernous space filled with light. In one direction, deep crevices pit the canyon walls. Balconies of coralline rock extend from the mouths of some of the crevices. Tendrils of red tree-like things wave at the entrances to them.

Another wall of balconies stretches out over Ra'Ook's shoulders. A cluster of faces like Ra'Ook's come into focus. They watch us as they swim out of darkness to the edge of their balconies. Sweeping tendrils of hair flow behind them, and their broad shoulders arch back as their round black eyes fix on me. There are so many of them now I can't count. They look surprised. I shift myself in Ra'Ook's grip to free a hand so I can wave, but his arms are immovable. His chest tightens against me like a stone. These marine people are growing in numbers as we rise up through the water. Some of them reach out to me, and Ra'Ook turns me away from them. His hold on me is fierce and crushing.

An angry face lunges toward me from the side, flashing purple to red and white. Ra'Ook spins me out of reach, but I catch a glimpse of black hair standing up into a fan and one black spine extending just barely along the edge of a thick forearm. I squelch my fear mid-scream. I can't look scared. I have to stay calm. *Ra'Ook, please protect me.* I want so desperately to be right in trusting him.

When I remember to look at my gauge, we're at 30 feet. My air is almost half gone. My computer readout says we began this dive three minutes ago and plunged to 210 feet. I have just survived the SCUBA equivalent of a sprint up Mount Everest without special gear. It's been done before. Extreme divers do it for thrills. They call it bounce diving. A quick descent to ridiculous depths on scuba just to see how far you can go before bouncing back up to the surface. Some of them never come back.

I push away from Ra'Ook enough to see his face. The hues beneath his skin pulse like ripples of red light penetrating a stormy sea. I point up with my thumb, and we swim to the surface. We emerge from the water into a spacious cavern. Stars appear to shimmer on the ceiling and cast a blue light over a breathtaking scene. The walls gleam with a rich, golden hue. In one corner, water flows along a path of bright green vines. "Come," Ra'Ook says, swimming to the edge of the water. He pulls himself partly onto the shore and rests on his side, the upper half of his body propped up on one elbow. His other half, his tail, gently sweeps the surface of the water.

The cave floor ends abruptly at the edge of deep water. I

kick myself onto dry land as if climbing out of the deep end of a pool. I remove my mask from my face, and it hangs from the hose in front of me like a metal bucket. My bulky gear is heavy and clumsy, but I finagle myself into a seated position with my legs dangling in the water. Something soft that looks like white moss covers the floor of the cave, stretching behind us to a semi-circle of rounded coral boulders. They rise like stairs to a far wall covered in a colorful array of blossoms. The air is surprisingly fresh and cool. Near one of the boulders, beneath a canopy of feathery white ferns, a tail moves. Then another.

The air echoes with a high pitched screech, and heads emerge from the water. Ra'Ooks. Dozens of them. Some of the faces are small with very narrow ridges and enormous eyes. Some of them reach taller out of the water with long necks and slender shoulders. Most are thick-chested like Ra'Ook but larger with sharp features. There are so many of them. All shifting between iridescent shades of red and purple. All swaying rhythmically. Serrated teeth visible in their snarling, half-open mouths. I pull my legs up and slide back. A deep rumble emanates from Ra'Ook's chest, and the heads sink a few inches. Now, they stare at me with their eyes just barely above the water. Ra'Ook has been lying on his side, leaning on one elbow. Now, he places both hands on floor and pushes himself up. With a loud slap of his tail, he propels his whole body onto dry land beside me. Propped up by his strong arms, he holds his head and shoulders tall.

Out of the water, he is enormous, powerful, and awkward. With my eyes glued to the sight of him—his silky tail glimmering in the blue light surrounding us—I don't notice them crowding in on me. When I do, there are dozens of them. Out of water, I see it and wonder why I hadn't realized it before. I was so shocked by him. So focused on understanding

Ra'Ook as a new species, or a mutant of Barru Pi's, it didn't register. But I see it now. They are not just marine-people. They're the mermaids and mermen of childhood stories. Dozens of mer-people. All loping toward me with long undulating movements of their tails.

One reaches toward me, the spines along his forearm alert and ready to strike. I lean closer to Ra'Ook. He glares at the faces around us, and they stop advancing.

"What are we doing here?" I grip his arm closer. "Are they going to kill me?"

"Not if I am here," he says. "This is my city."

This was a bad idea. Minutes ago, I had hoped to meet his father, the ambassador. I thought I would be welcomed. I thought they would be as excited for this contact as I am. But these . . . these merpeople are so threatening. They're not like Ra'Ook.

"Why are they so angry?" I ask.

"They have not seen air people. They only know your ways. Many of us killed. Our homes poisoned. We live safe here. But only here."

"Why would you bring me here?" I ask him.

"You come to our waters. I see your home. Now you see us," he answers.

"Can we go back, now?" I plead, trying not to look panicked. There is a splash in the water next to us. A small Ra'Ook pops up smiling at me with deep doe eyes. A child, maybe, with a narrow face and thin wisps of feathery hair. A girl, I think. She slides herself out of the water and rests on the ledge. Her face is the same lovely blue and green that Ra'Ook's was before we came here. Ra'Ook makes a screeching sound that sends the others into the shadows. The little girl reaches out of the water and touches my hair. I bend toward her and she places her fingers on my nose. Then she pokes her finger into one of my nostrils, and I jerk away. She whistles and squeals like a dolphin. I think she is laughing.

"Sister," Ra'Ook says, touching her shoulder. "RahEee."

She pokes in my ears. Looks at my feet. When I take off my fins, her eyes grow big and she clicks and squeals in surprise.

RahEee puts her hand up, palm toward her face, and says, "RahEee." Then she turns her palm to me and presses it toward my face.

"Alannis," I say. When she repeats, it sounds like All ' sss.

Ra'Ook puts my fin back on my foot and takes hold of my elbow. We slip into the water. "Now, I bring you home Al'Anss," he says to me. I survived the dangerous trip once, but I'm afraid this time it will kill me. This cave has to be inside one of the islands. There must be a way out onto land without diving to the bottom.

"Ra'Ook, Please. I can't go that way. It's too dangerous for me. Isn't there a way I can get out over land?"

"This is the way out if you want to return home." I have no choice but to go with him.

This time, I wrap both arms around his chest and bury my face into him. I close my eyes and focus all my energy on breathing calmly and slowly. The descent is a struggle between wakefulness and sleep. I am in that place between the two, wanting to rest, willing myself not to.

When we reach the surface, my head has cleared, but my tank is nearly empty. I will not make it back on the air that's left. Ra'Ook tells me it will be slower if we travel above the water, but it's the only way.

He glides on top of the water with me clinging to his back. My head rests between his shoulder blades. Exhaustion washes over me, and the steady rhythm of his movements pulls me unwillingly down into sleep. Suddenly, he stops and rolls me off. He gestures at the *Sun Joule* in the distance. I have never been so happy to see a boat before. Behind her, to the east, a sliver of orange light paints a line between the sea and the dawn sky. There is probably enough air for me to return on scuba, so I put my face mask back on and begin to descend. Ra'Ook says he will swim me right beneath the boat.

I'm about to put my arms around him when I remember. "Wait, I need to know if you can help us with something. Do you know how to stop the thing you call the black death?"

Ra'Ook's face darkens and his eyes narrow. He looks. . . hurt. "We return you now. We will not talk about your war."

"But I don't know anything about a war. If you know how to stop it, you have to tell me. Please."

He stretches a hand in the direction of the *Sun Joule.* "We swim?" he says. I suppose if I say no, he will leave me here to swim on my own. It's not far, but I wrap my hands around his neck and he carries me swiftly until we are right beneath the boat. I watch him swim away, back to his home. To all those angry mers who might have killed me if he had let them.

CHAPTER 18

I CAN ONLY HOPE EVERYONE IS STILL ASLEEP WHEN I HAUL myself onto the swim platform. Before I reach the platform, my eyes focus on Jake swimming around the boat. I forgot about Jake; he's been waiting all this time. He's switched to a standard regulator, and he's pretending to scrub the waterline which doesn't need scrubbing. I surface within inches of him.

He drops his brush and places his hands on either side of my bulky full-face mask. He lets out a long heavy breath, lifting his chin to the sky. The regulator falls from his mouth. "Alannis," he sighs. "I didn't know what I was supposed to do. What if you didn't come back?" Seawater drips down his face. Inside his mask, tears pool at the corners of eyes.

"I made it back. I'm fine now. I saw them…all of them."

Jake doesn't care right now. He wants me back on the boat. "They'll be up soon," he says anxiously. "What would I have told them if you didn't come back? I didn't even know where to look for you."

But there's no time to answer him. Guillermo calls out to us from the lower deck. "We are up early today, my friends." I dive below the boat, hoping he didn't see my full-face mask. Jake's lower body struggles to stay steady while he signals me with his hands underwater. It's a random assortment of gestures that makes no sense to me. But I can't stay down here like this.

I swim to the stern and climb onto the swim platform as quickly and quietly as possible. Guillermo and Jake's voices are muffled, but Jake is speaking loud enough for me to hear them. The bulky mask is attached to the air hose. I don't have the time or the tool to replace it with a standard regulator. I need to get this gear off and hide it before Guillermo sees it.

I almost have the full face mask and hoses disconnected from my tank when Jake calls out, "Alannis, where'd you go?" Guillermo must be on the move. I throw my gear, tank and all, into the locker in the floor of the deck. It slams shut just as Guillermo reaches the back deck. "Ah, we thought we had lost you," he booms. "Why such a hurry that you leave your dive buddy to swim alone?"

"Hungry," I say shaky with adrenalin "I thought he was behind me." I scurry around frantically putting away my fins hoping he doesn't notice there's a BC and regulator missing from the gear hooks

When Jake reaches the platform, I take his fins and mask, and he climbs aboard. Without giving him a chance to speak, I push right past both of them. "I'm starving. I'm glad you're up Guillermo. I wanted to ask you to show me how to make that pork and egg omelet. Can you show me that now?"

"You guys go on," Jake says shooting a look of relief my way. He knows what to do. When he's alone back here, Jake will put a standard regulator back on my air hose and shift my empty tank to the back row with the spares. I hope he remembers to clear my dive computer.

Lacey glares at me when Guillermo and I enter the galley. Until now, it hadn't occurred to me that Jake wasn't the only one wondering where I was. I didn't return to the cabin last night. I know how this might look to her, and I wish I could just tell her to get off my back. But that wouldn't be fair.

Instead, I give her a little hug and whisper, "It's not what you think, really."

I can't fight it anymore. By noon, it will be common knowledge: Alannis didn't sleep in her cabin last night. It's true, and I can't hide that. In a way, I'm almost thankful to Jake for putting this imaginary romance in their minds. There is no need to explain myself as I go to my cabin to get some rest. I lie on my bunk staring out the porthole. Something amazing happened last night, and they suspect nothing. If my reputation is the price I have to pay for that, it's worth the cost.

*

It's mid-morning and the team is preparing to dive when Jake finds me in my cabin. He's furious. "Your computer said 210 feet," he barks. "Please tell me you didn't go to 210 feet."

I explain everything as quickly as I can, before asking for his help. I'm afraid to dive this morning. I went too deep, stayed too long, I don't want to get decompression sickness. It's like opening a bottle of soda in your bloodstream. They call it the bends because divers double over from pain when it happens.

Jake's concentration tells me he is making the same calculations in his head that I've already done over and over again. He knows it isn't safe for me to dive today. My blood has absorbed a lot of air already, and I need to give it time to work its way out before I start packing in more.

Underwater, the air you breathe is compressed, like oranges squeezed down to the size of ping pong balls. It gets into your bloodstream, and when you come up, it expands back again. If you give it time, the extra air is supposed to ease its way out as it passes through your lungs. It's as if the ping pong balls swell slowly back into oranges and spill easily out of a duffel bag. When you go deep and stay too long, you cram more air into your blood. It's like cramming the duffel bag too full with ping pong balls. As they expand into oranges, there is no time for them to spill out one by one. The bag explodes. Your blood fizzes with air bubbles that flow through your veins and lodge in your system. I wasn't at 210 feet long enough to overload my blood with air last night, but I'm sure I absorbed plenty. Jake and I both know it hasn't had time to work its way out slowly. If I do a couple long dives today, I'll just be packing in more compressed air, overloading my bloodstream. This could leave me permanently crippled with the bends.

"You need to draw the line," Jake says. "You're mesmerized by him."

"I'm not mesmerized," I say. But then, I wonder, maybe I am. I know I need to be more careful.

"You're imagining some kind of connection. It's the siren call," Jake says, surprising me with his reference to the myth. "Wake up, Alannis. He's dangerous. If anyone goes with him, it should be me from now on."

So, that's what it's about. I have had the chance to explore and find out about Ra'Ook and his people while Jake has stayed behind. "You're jealous," I say.

"Jealous?" he yells back. "Of what, your fishboy?"

I rush toward him and put my hand over his mouth before someone hears him. It was a strange thing to say. Why would Jake be jealous of Ra'Ook?

Jake pries my hand from his mouth. "You can't have those feelings for him," he whispers. "He is a dangerous animal, and you shouldn't follow him into his lair."

"Just because he's not like us, you make him out to be an animal," I hiss. "He's an intelligent, thinking person."

"He's not a person," Jake says. "He belongs in an

aquarium."

"Don't even come near me." If I don't get away now, I'll shove him off the side of the boat. I turn and run back to the aft deck with the others.

I'm not sure what just happened. Jake is acting jealous. Not envious, but jealous. That doesn't even make sense. I can't really have some kind of feelings for Ra'Ook. The contrast between them comes to me in an instant. Jake and his sun-golden skin, the curve of his biceps, the definition in his chest and shoulders. Ra'Ook with those same muscular curves beneath his beautiful silky skin that shows his emotions in a kaleidoscope of color. Jake with his sincere blue eyes making me promise to return. Ra'Ook with his fierce strength carrying me home from the edge of death. It's an awkward, ridiculous flash of uncontrolled thought. An accident. But it makes me uncomfortable.

Divers are gearing up, and I'm scrolling through possible excuses like contacts on a phone. I could get seriously bent if I can't come up with something quick. Jake has come around to the deck from the other side. Without looking at me, and without a note of apology, he explains that I didn't sleep last night, and I need to rest. It is the truth, of course. I didn't sleep, but as he says this, I have to grit my teeth to bear what the others are thinking. I had finally earned a little bit of respect when Candace trusted me to keep the logs. Now she thinks I'm sleeping off a long night with the first mate. I glance at her expecting her to roll her eyes or shake her head. But she doesn't flinch. No acknowledgement at all, and that's far worse.

Once they're all in the water, though, I have to admit I am relieved. Sully has gone to the wheelhouse, and I'm left alone to reflect on the last few days. I'm witnessing something no one else can imagine. I am learning about an entire race of people that have remained hidden for millennia. By the time they return from the dive, I am well past caring what everyone else thinks of me.

*

By two in the morning, Jake finds me on the swim platform. I swore to him I wouldn't dive tonight, and I don't plan to go in. I've agreed to give myself a little distance from Ra'Ook. Get some perspective. Besides, I'm not up for another deep water adventure just yet. Ra'Ook and I can talk fine right here.

My feet dangle in the water. I have not set up our dive gear, but I do have a snorkel and fin beside me. Just in case. Jake picks them up and puts them away. I look toward the lights of those ominous submarines, beyond which the ocean seems to stretch forever.

Jake doesn't understand what this is. He still thinks of Ra'Ook as an animal. He hasn't felt what it's like to really communicate with Ra'Ook, to trust him. It occurs to me that Ra'Ook and I form a bridge between my people and his. I close my eyes and feel our hands palm to palm in front of us, the moon reaching through the water, reflecting the beauty of his iridescent skin. I can see where the legends come from. Sirens who lure sailors into the depths.

It's clear now. The legends are all true. Mermaids and mermen. Sirens. Maybe even the kraken and the Cubbarros Triad mysteries. There is truth behind them all. Guillermo's people knew this, and so did Barru Pi. Maybe she wasn't crazy at all.

We wait while the moon yawns across the sky. But Ra'Ook never comes.

CHAPTER 19

JAKE IS VISIBLY RELIEVED TODAY. HE THINKS RA'OOK HAS gone for good. I remind him that we may need Ra'Ook to show us how to stop the Fouling—if that is even possible at this point. But Jake thinks we have the answer right here, in the lab. Matt announced this morning that Jake's slimy algae is actually some sort of bacteria. When we return to the base, he'll collect more Fouling and run an experiment to see if the bacteria eats it. Jake's confidence is up. "This is what we came here to find," he says boldly to Dirk who raises his eyebrows and says with a glimmer of hope, "We'll see, Little J."

All day we stick to our routine, but the whole team is on edge, preoccupied by the feeling that we're failing in our mission. Just four days ago, when we left the Commission base and Lacey and Dirk updated us on the Fouling, the news was so grim that I wonder if it's not too late already. Even if we find something to stop the Fouling, we can't undo the damage that's already been done. We could give up and go home, but no one wants to face what's waiting there. I don't even want to think about home right now. All I want is to find Ra'Ook again. The sun can't set fast enough for me today.

When evening finally comes, I shuffle around the compressor, thankful for at least one thing. There are no extra tanks to fill behind Dirk's back. He and Lacey sit at the bow, listening to music on her tablet, and I'm dawdling here, waiting for them.

Then, Lacey yells out, "The squid are back, come look."

I run to the bow and Matt rushes up on deck. "You can see their tentacles pulsing with each stroke," he says. It's hard to see anything but streaks of light. They're not Ra'Ook, though. And they're not his people. Lacey says they definitely look like giant squid, and Dirk agrees.

I look for Guillermo, but he is not on deck. If they're his perrorap, he won't be joining us to look at them. His fears are no longer superstitions to me. Maybe they are perrorap. Maybe they're the kraken that Matt is so delighted by.

Sully runs to the wheelhouse and shuts the door behind him. When he returns, I'm shocked to see he has a spear gun in his hand. But he's too late. The squid are gone.

"Calamari," Dirk says, hanging over the rail to find them. "We could have calamari for breakfast."

"Yeah, right?" Lacey says, "That sounds appetizing, a three hundred pound squid. Who's going to cut that up and serve it for breakfast?"

"Shoot it with that little thing?" Matt chimes in looking at the large weapon in Sully's hand. "It would drag you down and serve you to the baby krakens for breakfast."

Dirk slaps Sully's shoulder. "Kraken slayer." Then he turns to me and says, "Gerry was terrified these things were going to track us down and kill us all. Had it in his head they had seen you on your little swim with your boy there." His choice of words grates on me, but what he's saying hits me hard.

"But you won't let them touch us," I mumble remembering his conversation with Guillermo on the bow. "You've got his back."

Dirk chuckles, "Looks like Sully's got his back now."

Dirk is truly a jerk, and that's all. He's no agent. The Commission isn't following us because of me. Dirk is a jerk who thinks he's here to save everyone. . .save Guillermo from the perrorap squid, save me from being homesick. He probably started going to the bow to save Lacey from sunburn. I burst out in laughter that's full of relief. Lacey looks at me as if I've gone over the deep end. If she only knew.

After we fill the tanks, Jake corners me at the door of my cabin. He pushes his way in and asks, "We're not going tonight. Your fishboy isn't coming back. Not with those things in the water."

I wish he would stop calling Ra'Ook my fishboy. Then a terrible thought strikes me. Ra'Ook is fierce and strong, and it took nothing for him to destroy a shark. But there are so many giant squid or perrorap, whatever they are. I imagine a swarm of tentacles and vicious beak-like jaws. "What if you're right? What if he never comes back?"

"Maybe that would be a good thing." Jake sounds tired. "If they have been around as long as he says, we should just leave them alone. Besides, I already know what controls the Fouling."

"How do you know for sure?"

"Before this trip, whenever my father and I went to sea, the first stage of the Fouling always accumulated on the hull. But when we arrive here from some place that has the Fouling, like Florida or the base, all we find on the bottom of the boat is that algae-like slime. Don't you see, we bring that very early stage of Fouling with us, but the bacteria attacks it. That's why it only accumulates for the first day or two. The bacteria eat it all. There is nothing left to build up on the hull."

"We need to ask Ra'Ook," I say.

"That hasn't worked out very well so far, has it?" Jake

retorts. "If Ra'Ook even knows about a control for the Fouling, he can't give us the data we need. We need to prove it with science. Let's just worry about getting to the base with you alive so Matt can run that experiment."

"So you want us to just forget about everything? Turn our backs on all of this and go home to our regular lives?"

"No, we definitely can't do that," he barks. "Because you're forgetting—I don't have a regular life to go back to. My life is upside-down enough. I don't need to make friends with the Commission's deadly secrets. And I don't need to watch that thing carry you off into the ocean again."

It never occurred to me to think how that must have looked. How it must have felt to watch someone disappear into black ocean with an alien creature and not return for hours. Jake doesn't deserve what's happened to him this whole year. No one does. I understand now that I'm risking more than my own life when I go with Ra'Ook. Jake has been standing beside me, bearing the weight of our secret, too.

I suddenly want to do something to help him. I realize how much I'll miss him when we go our separate ways. Maybe my father can get him a scholarship to Braverton. He could stay with us, in the au pair's room. My dad could hire Sully to captain one of the university's research vessels. Except, there may be no more research vessels if the Fouling doesn't stop.

Jake turns to walk away, but I find myself taking his hand. He turns to face me, and I lean forward to kiss his cheek. "It's going to work out," I say. "Somehow, everything will be alright."

His tense shoulders loosen as he puts his arms around me. We relax into a hug. His warm skin is comforting and soothing. I feel safe with Jake. He is safe. I think that's why I push him away sometimes.

When he leaves, my narrow, low ceilinged, claustrophobic bunk is a welcome refuge from the fatigue closing in on me. I don't have any idea what time it is when I wake. Afraid I have been asleep too long, I rush up on deck to look over the rail. A faint glow shoots by the boat. It must be deep because it's almost imperceptible. I wonder where Ra'Ook is. Did he try to come back? Was he attacked?

Not sure what's down there, I hold a fin over the edge and gently tap the water with it. Gradually, the light grows closer. His tail lights the water in undulating streaks that grow brighter as he nears. It's him.

"My Ra'Ook!" The outburst surprises me. Not *my* Ra'Ook. Just Ra'Ook.

Jake's called him "mine" so often, I guess it has taken hold. He is mine in a way. Jake barely spoke with him. He and Ra'Ook still see each other as inferior animals. I don't see Ra'Ook as an animal at all. He's not all that different from us. Watching him light the water beneath the boat, I'm anxious to see him surface. I imagine jumping in and dashing off with his arms tightly around me. I push away the danger in my mind. It's not a danger that comes from Ra'Ook's strong grip or fierce claws. It comes from my own desire to trust him, and to get to know him. It grows more dangerous every day.

When he lifts his head from the water, I reach toward him. "Why didn't you come last night?" I say. "I was so worried."

Ra'Ook waves me into the water. No one is here to stop me. I can't stop myself.

"ShaOhm is angry. He tells me. I should not bring you to our city. He forbids me to come to you." Behind Ra'Ook, one of those giant squid things zooms in the distance. I instinctively grab Ra'Ook and try to pull him toward the boat, but when he turns around to look at them, he just smiles.

"My guard dogs," he says.

"Your what?" I ask.

"This is what your people call them."

One of them speeds toward me close enough to see—a frightening seal-like face with large saber teeth. Ra'Ook throws out his arm, and the animal turns away. A tangle of tentacles propels the long body past me. A yellow flash, and it's gone.

"They are sentries," he says. "They protect us and warn us from. . . well, they are like your horn. My father has insisted they stay with me always now."

"What horn?" I ask.

"The siren you send from your home when you swim." How odd it sounds to hear him describe this boat as our home. I don't know if I can ever fully see myself through his eyes. "It hurts our ears and drives our dogs away," he says.

I have a vision of Sully emerging from the wheelhouse last night with a spear gun in his hands and the squid already gone. His words, "I have magic of my own" ring in my ears as I think back to the dives when we felt like we were being watched. When Sully began spending time in the wheelhouse, the presence disappeared.

It's an alarm. Sully has been keeping Ra'Ook and the perrorap-squid away with an acoustic alarm—the ultra-high frequency kind that human's can't hear. Fishermen use them to keep dolphin out of their nets. How much does Sully know?

"My father believes I led a spy into our home," Ra'Ook says, "but I do not agree." His eyes will not meet mine. "I question now because you ask me if I know how to stop the black death. Will you tell me this is not true? Why are you here?"

"Spy for what?" I ask. "No one is spying on you, no one

even knows about you. Well, maybe somebody knows about you, but I don't know who they are. None of my people know about your people."

Ra'Ook looks furious. His skin subtly shifts between orange and purple. "Your people destroy our homes for more than one hundred years. They drown us in their nets and poison us with their dirty rivers. They kill our food. We are nearly gone, and you turn your heads. You pretend we don't exist."

I shake my head. "I'm sorry. It's not like that."

"It is like that," he flashes. "We are now only small numbers. Small territories. You make your treaty to leave us alone, and still your people send us the black death."

"The Fouling?" I say. "It's killing our people, too. It's everywhere, crusting up entire harbors and sinking ships. It's destroying our coasts. We're here to find a solution."

Ra'Ook looks just as confused now as I am. "This Fouling, you call it. This is not the black death."

"Yes, it is. That's what I'm talking about. The black encrusting organism that's all over this ocean. Everywhere but here."

"It is not here because it is ours. A reply to your attack."

"What attack?" I ask.

"The black death you spew from the pipes and leak from your fallen cities."

Oil? He's talking about oil. "Did you think we were not prepared?" he continues. "Your people spit black death everywhere. Now you fill the sea with it. My father plans many years for this attack. Do you think we do not attack back?"

The hairs stand up on the back of my neck at the words "attack back." Ra'Ook's father spread the Fouling on purpose. It IS a weapon.

"You're wrong," I tell him. "There was an oil spill. Many of our people suffered, too. It was an accident. It was not an act of war. We're here to find a way to stop the Fouling. That's all."

"Prove this accident," he says. "Many years we battle and negotiate. How is it you do not know we exist? Are you so blind?"

We have been blind. Not only to the Commission's secret, but perhaps to the rulers of Cubbarros as well. Centuries of dictators who were said to be superstitious and insane. But somehow they were undefeatable. Were they the only ones who knew the real truth?

Maybe their myths are true. Maybe all of them are. What does that mean for the stories we've believed? Are they just lies, the real myths? Like Guillermo said, the truth doesn't matter. What matters is what people will believe. We have all been completely blind.

Ra'Ook tells me his father will continue to send the Fouling along the coasts. There are small communities of his people around the world who will spread it until every shore is covered.

I stumble to speak, "I thought you were the only ones."

"The only ones here," he replies. "Far away oceans, others are safe in small places. Like us."

"I need to think." I move closer to him and see a flash below me. I reach my hands up to face him, and as our finger tips touch we press our palms together. Such a fragile connection.

"Think," he says. "We think now. Talk tomorrow."

He moves away from me, swimming backward, his hand still held up, palm facing me. He is so human. Even with his graceful tail and unusual face. Does he see me the same way?

So like him with my strange legs and awkward breathing gear?
We watch each other as he disappears into blackness.

CHAPTER 20

I WAKE JAKE AND TELL HIM WHAT RA'OOK SAID. I EXPLAIN that Ra'Ook's people think we are trying to destroy the oceans. That we are trying to kill them with oil spills. "They think we are attacking them on purpose," I say. "They sent the Fouling to stop us."

"I told you he was dangerous," Jake hisses. "We should head straight for those submarines and tell them to blow these fish people out of the water."

His fear and anger disgust me. They are the emotions of war, maybe the very war Ra'Ook's people are fighting against. If Guillermo is right, when we leave, the submarines will do exactly what Jake's suggesting. Ra'Ook and his people will be gone, and the world will never know it.

"The Fouling was a mistake," I argue. "ShaOhm wouldn't have sent it if that massive oil spill hadn't happened last year. It's all a misunderstanding." He knows I'm right. His face softens as it sinks in. We have to find a way to end this secret war. "This is bigger than the two of us," he says. "We need help."

My first instinct is to tell Sully, but it would be a mistake now that I know about the horns. Sully must know about all of this, but Jake refuses to believe he is a part of it. He will admit that his father is carrying around a lot of anger since everything happened. If we told Sully the truth, he might be angry enough

158

to wipe out Ra'Ook's people himself.

Between Lacey and Dirk's attraction to drama, Guillermo's fear of the legends, and Matt's fascination with them, we agree Candace is our best bet. She may be the one person who can look at things in a completely analytical light, without emotion. We'll tell her tomorrow at the first opportunity.

All day, I try to get Candace alone in a quiet space, but it doesn't work. She's constantly within earshot of someone else. Anyway, each time I get close, I stumble with my words. It becomes clear we can't just tell her. She would think the whole story was crazy. Somehow, we have to introduce her to Ra'Ook.

Sully and Candace are late in joining the rest of us for dinner. Sully sits down next to Lacey and rests his elbows heavily on the table. "We just got a call on the satellite phone. The Fouling's caked all over oil rigs in the gulf of Oman, halfway around the world. A couple of ships have gone missing in the Pacific."

Candace walks slowly toward us. "We're going home. They pulled the plug."

"I'm sorry,' Dirk says. "I don't think there's anything I can do." Dirk's agency the National Oceanographic Invasive Species Institute funded this expedition, so I guess he thinks he's supposed to have the power to keep the money flowing.

"We had to know it was coming," Candace says weakly. "It is relatively clear our work here is futile. The Fouling cannot be stopped. The agency's new strategy is to try to overcome. To quickly develop and build oil-free technologies that the Fouling won't harm."

"That will take decades," Matt says, "Maybe longer."

159

"If it's even doable, it will be too late for most people," Sully adds. I know what he means. It will be too late for him, and for everyone who has lost their livelihood to the Fouling. It may be too late for all of us.

Candace doesn't pick up a plate and serve herself dinner. She doesn't sit. She just looks each of us in the eyes. "Early tomorrow we'll gather our equipment on the seafloor and leave by mid-morning." She turns away and retreats to her cabin. It's over.

Absolute silence fills the boat. We have been living in a bubble out here, believing we could find a solution. The serenity of this untouched reef has made it easy to ignore the truth. In some way, we have grown into an awkward kind of family. We're going to need each other to face the ride home.

"They will have their revenge," Guillermo says, the rims of his eyes welling with tears. He turns his head away to scan the ocean. "Such majesty," he sighs sweeping his hand out in a broad semi-circle in front of him.

After dinner, Jake and I whisper on the dive platform, as the compressor roars behind us. Lacey and Dirk fill scuba tanks for tomorrow morning.

"We can't leave," I say desperately.

"It's too late," Jake replies.

"But, they'll destroy the reef."

"Probably," he agrees, "and the bacteria we came to find."

That's exactly it. "Jake, all we need is to know for sure if that's what stops it," I say urgently. "Ra'Ook knows. He has to. Even if he can't stop the Fouling, he must know what does."

"Yeah, I know, too," he says, "but what good does knowing do if we can't get the job done?"

"It can buy us time to figure something out," I answer. "If Candace announces that we found the control, no one will want us to just pack up and leave."

"And how will we get Candace to announce that? They didn't even want to look at the stuff until I shoved it under their noses."

Of course the answer is obvious. "She may not take you or me seriously," I beam at him, "but she won't be able to ignore Ra'Ook."

I hope I am right. At two in the morning, Jake and I meet on the aft deck to set up the gear. Two full face mask rigs— that's all there are on the boat—and one regular scuba rig.

My legs dangle off the swim platform, gently slapping the water's surface with my fins. If Ra'Ook is here, he will know I'm waiting for him. When his "guard dogs" flash around beneath me, I jerk my legs up and wait for him.

His head has barely broken the surface of the water when I begin to talk. "Stay here," I plead. "We have someone who can help us. Please trust me."

All of the anxiety I felt the first time I met Candace Warren floods through me again. I stand at her cabin door taking shallow, shaky breaths. I hope my knock will wake her and no one else. I raise my knuckles and tap gently.

Nothing. Again. Still nothing. I'm afraid to tap louder, so I gently open her door with a trembling hand and step inside.

"Dr. Warren," I say. Instinctively reverting to formality.

She wakes with jerk and bolts out of bed. "What is it?" she says, grabbing a sweater from a hook beside her bunk. "What is it? What's happened?" She rushes out the door and leaps up the stairs calling into the salon. "What's wrong?"

The salon is dark and empty, so she rushes out of the boat, and I run behind to keep up with her. When she sees

Jake on the back deck with the dive gear she stops short. She turns around to me and says, "What's going on?"

I press toward her, urging her, "Shhh, Candace Please."

Jake whispers loudly to us, "Candace, there's something important we need to show you."

Ra'Ook's head and shoulders hover out of the water next to the platform. Candace's jaw drops, her hands fall to her sides. I think she might pass out, and Jake moves behind to catch her. While I suit up for a dive, Ra'Ook puts his hand up to Candace and calls out, "Come," in his croaky above-water voice. He dives and the guard dogs or perrorap, or whatever they are, streak all around him. Candace has not moved. She breathes in broken gulps, making stiff gasping noises as her chest convulses in and out. Jake takes one of her hands and leads her closer to the platform. The swish of air from my gear rings out.

Candace lurches forward. "Don't!"

"It's OK," I say before sliding under. I swim to Ra'Ook and take hold of his left hand. When we surface I raise our clasped hands into the air so Candace will see. Jake is handing her a BC with a tank and full face mask. I don't think any of this has registered yet. Her body is stiff, her eyes wide, jaw still hanging open.

"Candace," I say, "this is about the Fouling. About the Commission and the submarines." She's shaking her head, no. "I know it's a lot to deal with. But we don't have time. We need your help. Please."

Ra'Ook puts his elbows on the platform and rests his head on his arms. His tail lights the water as it waves slowly back and forth.

Jake and I tell her everything. As I explain it, Ra'Ook hears for the first time about the legends of sirens and mermaids, about giant squid-like kraken and perrorap, and stories of aliens and ships lost mysteriously in the Cubbarros Triad. I tell Candace we have all been fooled with more than a century of lies about fictitious wars with Cubbarros, crazy dictators, and toxic experiments run amok. I explain the misunderstanding over the oil spill and the Fouling.

She has been staring at Ra'Ook the whole time. "What do you want?" she asks him.

"Peace," he replies.

After some urging, Candace lets Jake help her quickly and quietly into her diving gear. Beneath the water Candace stares at Ra'Ook's tail.

"Show us what stops it," I beg him. "We have to know."

Jake is impatient beside me. Without a full face mask, his regulator turns his words into a garbled moan. He tugs on my elbow, and makes broad circles with his hand as if he is scrubbing the bottom.

"It's the slime on the bottom of the boat isn't it?" I ask Ra'Ook.

Ra'Ook mimics Jake's hand movement. "I see you do this," he snarls toward Jake. "You are not smart to wipe away what keeps you floating." Jake glowers back as him.

Candace looks at Jake. "We need data," she says. "We can't confirm anything without data."

"But you can tell them we have to run an experiment at the base," I say.

"There is no time," she answers. "I can't suddenly announce I have found a control without evidence."

"Return to dead city," Ra'Ook cuts in.

The shipwreck. He called it that before. This time, I see it through his eyes. A sunken ship filled with hundreds, maybe thousands of humans. Dead city now seems the perfect way to describe it.

"This Fouling, the crust as you call it, consumes the black death that spills from your broken city. This slime," he continues, wiping his hand in circular motions, "it consumes the crust." Ra'Ook's hands move up and down in the water like a seesaw. "They balance. Go there and see. It will prove what you want. But you will not stop it. The crust will cover your land where it meets every ocean."

"Can you make your father stop it?" I ask him.

"My father is ShaOhm. He can stop it and more," he says. "There is enough to take away the crust in a few moon cycles. But I do not know where the farms are." I feel a shiver at the word "farms." Jake and I look at each other. Ra'Ook and his people are more advanced than I imagined. "My father will never show you. He believes you are here to destroy us."

"Then we need to prove otherwise," Candace says without flinching. I'm amazed by how quickly she has pulled herself together and is getting straight to the business of solving the problem. "If we can convince him that the oil spill was an accident, would he have the ability to stop the Fouling?"

Ra'Ook shakes his head. "Because you say this? No. We are not so easy to fool. How will you prove these things to him?"

We can't, of course. Even if we could, we're leaving in the morning.

"Next night, bring proof. Show me where there are others who want peace," Ra'Ook says. "Maybe there is a chance." He leaves us before we can respond. He doesn't know it, but with those subs out there, finding a solution to the Fouling may be his only chance, too.

CHAPTER 21

WE SCRAMBLE TO DOFF OUR DIVE GEAR AND PUT IT AWAY before dawn breaks. Candace is silent. She won't look at us. Perhaps she is processing everything that has been thrown at her in the last few hours. When everything is put away, we stand on the back deck, looking at each other blankly. What is there to say?

"Evidence does not appear out of thin air," she says.

There's a sudden light in Jake's eyes. "It does," he says. "All it takes is a satellite and an Internet connection."

"But we don't have an internet connection," I say exasperated and unsure how that would help us anyway. "We can," he answers. "I can connect us through the satellite feed. We can download all the evidence we need from the web."

"The web," I repeat. "Brilliant." With pictures and videos, we could show Ra'Ook and his father how devastating the oil spill was on land. We could show him it was an accident, that there are people trying to protect the oceans.

The sun will be up soon, but we decide to download as much as we can onto Candace's laptop. Jake connects it to the satellite feed and we gather all the evidence we can. News reports showing the oil spill was an accident. Deep sea divers trying to patch the holes in the pipe. Oil company executives apologizing, and fishermen telling the camera how the spill damaged their businesses. We've downloaded an entire documentary on environmental recovery efforts that shows volunteers washing ducks and cormorants. Other documentaries show people rescuing beached dolphins and ships protecting whales from hunters.

We also want to show ShaOhm that, whoever he is dealing with, they're not the only ones on Earth. So, we find videos of people from as many different races and cultures as we can get.

The sky is beginning to lighten above us, and Guillermo's footsteps thud softly across the deck. He's up for his morning smoke. Candace sneaks down to keep him company, and to make sure he doesn't wander to the top deck.

Jake and I move on, searching for stories about Cubbarros. We're looking for videos or still pictures that show the history of the islands, and the myths and lies that people have believed in. As I'm looking through this material, I feel a twinge of guilt. Aside from taking notes on the species we've seen, I haven't written in my journal this whole trip. I've been too distracted to think about a school report, but now, as frivolous as it seems, the idea of blowing it off still worries me.

Candace has walked to the foredeck so we can see her. It's her signal that we need to wrap it up. The last things we manage to download include satellite shots of the earth and aerial videos of the Grand Canyon and the Amazon Jungle. We want to show them what the planet looks like far inland. If they have their own myths about humans and our world, I hope these videos will show them the truth.

The plan is to pack Candace's laptop in one of the waterproof microscope cases tonight and take it to Ra'Ook's father. Of course, getting the proof was the easy part. The team expects to leave in the morning. We're still not sure how to delay our departure. We made a half dozen plans to keep the boat from leaving. None of them seem very good. We talked about hiding an expensive piece of equipment underwater and pretending we couldn't find it. We thought we could leave a line hung up on the propeller shaft that might wrap up in the prop when the boat gets underway. As a last resort, if we can't work something else out, Jake is going to try to erase the charts from the navigation system.

Jake and I walk into the salon with the laptop hidden in a blanket, as if we've been up on deck together all night. Dirk and Lacey are making coffee in the galley. "Want a cup?" Lacey asks with obvious disgust in her voice. At least Candace finally knows what Jake and I were really doing all night.

The entire group is slow to assemble our gear for our last dive. No one wants to do this. Even Dirk is uncharacteristically quiet. Guillermo waits until we're on the back deck ready to dive. Then he makes a plea that changes everything for us.

"Why should we not take our time today?" he asks. "Beauty such as this. Fish this magnificent. These are the companions of my childhood. These, we may never see again." He pinches the end off a new cigar. I half-expect him to light it and jump in the water with it. But he just grips it at the base of two fingers and waves his hands in the air. "Our journey from here will be much longer than any of us knows. Please, my friends, stay with me in my homeland today, so that we may say our final farewell."

Thankfully, his appeal to the team strikes a chord. No one wants to deny him one last visit to the reef, and it seems like something we should all do together. We agree to collect our gear on the first dive. Then we'll dive the rest of the day just for the beauty of it. Dirk abandons me to buddy up with Lacey. I'm released from the sergeant's ranks, and the group simply assumes I will dive with Jake. I can't complain. I will finally be able to relax underwater.

Aside from working right into our plan, Guillermo's idea really is a good one. The mood is somber, but the reef has a settling effect. As we surface from each dive, we talk as if it were day one. Each of us throws our voice into the conversation, calling out names of fish once thought extinct and coral formations that took our breath away. It's a dream, but none of us are willing to wake from it yet.

On the last dive of the day, Jake and I descend through a small canyon of coral. I look up as a cloud of amber jacks disperses into a constellation of fish overhead. Seconds later, they contract into a unified mass, and move through the water as a single unit. Jake reaches out and takes my hand. We swim together through this magical reef understanding how much is at stake.

We've been down about a half an hour when I hear a strange humming sound. It grows louder until I recognize it as the sound of a motor. As we swim closer to the *Sun Joule*, the underside of an inflatable Zodiac comes into view. It's tied up alongside the boat.

We lift ourselves onto the platform, and I catch a glimpse of Lacey and Matt standing behind Guillermo with a stunned look on their faces. There is an argument on the top deck. Then two men stomp down the stairs with three laptops under their arms. Candace and Dirk follow closely behind.

The men hand the computers down to a third guy in the inflatable. All of them wear silver and black Commission uniforms.

"Dad, you can't let them take those," Jake yells out.

"It's not your concern." Sully's shoulders are squared and rigid.

"That's crazy. They need their computers," Jake continues

to argue. He's pushing a little too hard for something that doesn't belong to him.

"Stand down, Jake," Sully cuts him off. "I won't have any unauthorized activity jeopardizing this boat, period." There's no trace of that warm, grandfatherly look. Guillermo's arms hang limply at his sides. With his palms turned upward, he looks at his colleagues and lifts his shoulders slightly. There is nothing to say. It's as if he has given up the fight, and this is just one more blow.

The Commission officers leave with a final command for us to stay anchored until they've investigated our activity. When they're gone, Sully explains. The large unauthorized download to our satellite receiver early this morning raised their suspicions. They've confiscated all the computers for inspection. They want to know what we're up to. We should have realized the Commission submarines were monitoring everything.

It's hard to resist the urge to blurt out something in our defense. No one else says anything. Surprisingly, neither Sully nor the other scientists even ask who used the satellite link this morning, or why. With the Commission now involved, suspicion is running high between everyone on the boat, and the rest of the team is unwilling to dig for answers. We hardly speak to one another as we wait for word of our fate.

A group dinner seems out of the question, so Jake and I scrounge around the galley for leftovers. Matt has retreated to the lab, his constant refuge. Guillermo mills around the side of the boat, sucking and chewing his soggy cigar in place of dinner. Lacey and Dirk are eating on the back deck by the dive gear. I can only assume that Sully is in the wheelhouse, watching.

Jake and I pick at our plates without much appetite when

Candace asks if she can join us. It's odd to see her sit cross-legged next to me with her dinner plate nestled in her lap.

"I can tell them it was me," I say. "I downloaded all of that stuff for school."

"No one needs to say a word," Candace says. "We did not download classified or illegal information."

"But if they ask. I have a good excuse. I should have been working on a report this whole time anyway." I dread the thought of another interrogation by Commission men, but if it comes down to it, my story is the only one that makes sense.

Candace abruptly changes the subject. "What did your father do in the navy?" she asks Jake.

"He was an engineer," Jake answers. "He was a Navy SEAL, and then he went back to school and became an engineer."

"Do you think he could be involved with the Commission?"

Jake looks at her without answering.

"I'm not suggesting anything here," says Candace. "I'm just throwing out options."

"My father is a stern man, but he's honest. He wouldn't be part of the Commission. Did you forget they sink boats they don't like?" His tone is unusually biting, especially since he's speaking to Candace.

Jake might not want to admit it, but Sully knows about the perrorap. He has to be involved, I just don't know how. But it doesn't matter now anyway. We're leaving tomorrow, and we have no evidence for Ra'Ook.

I want to change the whole mood of the conversation, so I try to segue into more neutral territory. "What about your parents, Candace? Where they scientists?"

She straightens her shoulders. "My parents were farmers

in East Africa." I can't hide my surprise. "I came here with my aunt when I was six," she adds.

"That's cool, do you remember it?" Jake says. "Do you ever go back?"

"No," is all she says.

We push our food around our plates uneasily until it seems useless to stay out here. I go to my cabin to lie in my bunk and try to read. The words on the page are meaningless. I have to go see Ra'Ook tonight. I'll be empty-handed, I hope for a brief moment that he will take me to his father anyway. I want to try to convince him. It's a ridiculous thought. But still.

It must be close to midnight when Lacey finally returns to the cabin. I don't want to talk to her. I want her to go to sleep. She senses my mood and, misinterpreting it, tries to cheer me up with new stories from Dirk. It goes on and on. Even after she's undressed and gotten into bed, she's still talking. Finally, I can't take it. I have to shut her up.

"I don't care," I shout. "You and Dirk should be more worried about the Commission and what's on those laptops. Don't you even care that all that data is gone?"

"Not really," she says. "I have a backup on my tablet."

I sit up on my elbow. "You what?"

"I backed it up. When the Commission guys came on board, they told Sully to confiscate the laptops, and Dirk started arguing with them. While Sully was trying to cool them down, I ran to the lab and backed everything up." Lacey has been dying to tell this story. "They didn't ask about other devices, and I didn't offer," she says, lingering over her clever deception.

"Lacey, you're brilliant!" I scream jumping off my bunk. "I have to have it. Give me your tablet." I don't even wait for her response. I tear through her locker, grab the tablet, and run out of the cabin. "I'll be right back," I lie.

I rush to the lab, grab a dry bag, and throw the tablet in there. As I run to the back deck I see a faint light cascading down the steps from the wheelhouse. Sully's still up there. I grapple with my gear, trying to be as silent and quick as possible. Switching out my regulator for a full face mask will make too much noise, and there's no time. I assemble the regulator and tank, snap on a weight belt and shove my arms through my BC. I don't even bother to buckle it. Lacey will be dressed and on me in minutes.

The dry bag has a seal like a drysuit, and my fingers fumble with the zipper and the fold-over flap. Every move I make sounds to me like an elephant stomping, and I feel like this has already taken way too long. I grab my mask and fins and slide into the water. I'll put them on and buckle my BC once I'm in I haven't even checked to see if Ra'Ook is here, but I can't risk Lacey finding me, or Sully catching me in the water. I pull myself together, arrange my gear and swim quietly away from the boat, hoping Ra'Ook will see me. When he lifts his head out of the water, I hold the bag up to show him.

His eyes flash with surprise, and he darts away. Perrorap swarm around me, and Sully yells from the stern of the boat, "Get out of the water!" I turn just in time to see him shoot a spear over my shoulder. Behind him Lacey screams. A perrorap launches into the air, pummels into Sully, and lifts him right off the swim platform. I feel a sudden jerk on my leg and I'm dragged down into the water so fast my ears ring out in pain. All I can do is focus on holding my nose and swallowing until they clear.

On the bottom, Ra'Ook holds me down. A dim wavering starburst of moonlight surrounds his silhouette. His cheeks flash like fire beneath his skin. His hands press into my shoulders. His claws are out. The dry bag has fallen out of my hands. I reach around beside me, but it's too dark to see anything.

"I have proof," I try to tell him, but the regulator in my mouth keeps me from making any sense.

"You tried to kill me," he said. "You lie."

"No," I yell out, groping in the dark for my dry bag. His palm glows as he grasps it and holds it in front of my face.

"You bring me this? And a human shoots at me?" His growl is ferocious. He is not the Ra'Ook I thought he was. He lets go of me, but as I try to push myself off the bottom, he pulls me to him and takes off. He is speeding through the water, descending so quickly, I can't tell how far or how deep we are going in this blackness. He holds my arms tight against my sides, and I can't see my gages. I'm trapped. I don't know what I can do to get away from him. He's going to kill me.

My heart beats furiously, and my mind races too fast for me to focus. Images of my parents and my brother keep coming to me. *What if I never see them again? What if I disappear and they never know what happened?* I push the thought away. I'm not willing to go there. I have to survive this.

It's only my ears that tell me we're beginning to ascend again. Ra'Ook loosens his grip on me. No lights glimmer from balconied honeycombs. No distinct shapes to identify. Just bright white lights shooting by. They begin to swarm around my head, dive bombing me, but never quite touching. As they pass closely, they make a high pitch click that reminds me of bats hunting for insects on a summer night, the way they swoop in close, echo-locating on their prey. Then they're gone, and we are swimming through pitch black water. I have no frame of reference. It's a surprise to me when our heads break the surface.

CHAPTER 22

My eyes are still adjusting to the light when Ra'Ook hoists me up onto a hard, rocky surface. The floor of a cave, but not the colorful landscape of his home. This one is dark and empty. No vines drape themselves along gentle waterfalls. No warm light envelopes us. Cold stone walls pulse with a greenish glow that appears to slide down them like some sort of sludge.

Above me, pinpoints of light illuminate the low ceiling like a night sky full of stars. I can't tell what I'm looking at. Ra'Ook places the dry bag beside me.

"Evidence," he growls. "Where is your proof?"

My regulator falls from my mouth, and I push my mask over my head. I gag from a putrid smell filling my nose. My hands shake as I fumble with the dry bag, and Ra'Ook watches me unflinchingly. When I pull the tablet out, a small wave of relief ripples through me. It's dry. Seconds pass like hours while I wait for it to boot. Sully is dead. The scene flashes in front of me a thousand times a second. The look of horror on his face as that awful beast plunged into the water with him in its grip.

The tablet comes to life, and I search through Lacey's files for the right folder. The first thing Ra'Ook sees is a segment on people saving a beached dolphin. I show him a clip in which a whole village drills holes through a frozen bay to help a stranded whale find his way to the open ocean. Ra'Ook watches silently. His expression is unreadable. I show him an illustration of mythical mermaids and read the story that goes with it.

I worry about the battery, so I turn it off. "Let me show ShaOhm." I dread the thought of another high speed plunge through the dark, but I hope he will take me to see his father. Instead, he pushes away from me and disappears. I am alone.

I look down into the black water. From the rocky edge, the cave drops straight down into an abyss. There is no bioluminescence lighting Ra'Ook's path. Time churns forward one agonizing minute at a time. Maybe thirty minutes pass, and I am still alone. I begin to realize I can't just wait here for something to happen. My dive gear suddenly feels heavy on my back, and I realize I've been sitting here with it on.

For the first time, it occurs to me to check my computer for depth. My last dive was 180 feet. 60 yards. On land, I can run a 50-yard dash in under seven seconds. Here, descending blindly 60 yards through an unlit cave could be deadly. Divers get lost in caves half that deep. Anyway, even if I can find my way down and back to the surface again, what will I find there? Miles of empty ocean?

I remove my dive gear. Feeling the cool, damp air on my back. If only I had taken an extra minute to get in the water. If I had tried to put my mask and fins on while I was still on the boat, Lacey might have had time to stop me. Or Sully might have caught me before I went in. Maybe that would have been better. I look around, straining to see in the darkness. I should have told Candace about Lacey's tablet. I should have woken Jake. Mounds of rubble lie strewn around the ground. Fallen stalactites. Above me, I can barely make out their shapes, among the starry pinpoints of light. I watch the lights until they finally come into focus. They are glow worms hanging from the ceiling. Thousands of them spitting strands of mucous with little glowing pearls of gunk strung out like a necklace. I didn't really expect them to be stars, but I'm disappointed anyway.

Sully didn't have to die.

Along one wall of the cave, amidst the green slime, there seems to be a large area of darkness where nothing glows, perhaps a crack, a passageway out. I walk carefully toward it, but my foot strikes a piece of rubble. I trip and fall forward, land with my hands outstretched. Something breaks off as I grip.

A glove. Black. Neoprene. A dive glove! Oh my god, it's a hand. A person. The rubble beneath me is a diver. Bones, held together inside a crumbling wetsuit.

An empty dive mask stares at me, tangled in hair above white teeth and a jaw bone. My scream echoes, chasing me to the edge of the water. From one wall to the next, all around me, what I thought was rubble morphs into recognizable shapes. Bodies of divers. Some with their gear still on their backs. Some merely a huddle of bones curled into corners and held together with the last remnants of flesh. The gear looks old. Round black rubber masks and bulky BCs that look more like horseshoe-shaped life vests. I drop to my knees and gag over the water.

A splash startles me, and Sully is propelled halfway up onto the ground beside me. I haul him out of the water. Small eyes hover at the surface. It is RahEee. Ra'Ook surfaces next. He reaches for the dry bag, points at the tablet and says, "Put it in."

When he dives away with the bag, I reach for Sully. He is blue and limp, and I press my ear against his chest. There is nothing. I shake him. Still nothing. I straddle him and push on his chest over and over. I yell his name. Nothing happens. I throw my body over him.

"Sully," I gasp, "Sully, I'm sorry." Then something beneath him catches my eye.

Wetness. Blood. Bitten, perhaps, horribly wounded. I pull his shoulders over, trying to roll him on his side to see what's been done to him. He spews a flood of frothy white seawater all over me and begins coughing fitfully. He's alive. Oh god, Sully's alive.

Weakly, his hand reaches up to my side, and he opens his eyes in a daze. I rub his face, shake him, and call his name. Sully's alive, but he's not well. The air around us is thick with the smell of decay. I have to get him out of here.

I leave Sully lying on his side and force myself into the dark corner, hoping it will be a way out. I stumble over bodies and scuba tanks, walking my hands along the wall as I go. But the wall ends abruptly. A trickle of cold water runs down the corner, but nothing more. There is no gap, no crack through which I can find an escape. Above me there is nothing but smooth rock stretching over my head and out of reach. Way up at the top of this corner, I think I see the gray of a very distant light. A low rumble gives me the hope that it's more than just glowing slime. Waves. I try to still my breathing and listen. It's definitely waves crashing. There must be an opening up there. I search for a handhold, a place to grip, anything to help me scale the walls above me.

There is nothing but smooth wet rock. My moment of hope fades. A jolt of terror runs through me. The reality of the bones around me sets in. The image of all these divers doing exactly what I'm doing now.

Sully is where I left him, curled on his side and shaking. With his back to me, I get my first look at the bloody gash across his torso. I rip off part of his blood soaked t-shirt to press against it, but the wound is deep and doesn't stop seeping blood. He needs help, soon. I'm shivering, and my fingers burn with cold. I don't know how long ago all of this started, but Sully must have been in the water a couple of hours. He's wounded, cold, and losing body heat. Looking around the cave, my eyes linger over the wetsuits that lie strewn around us. Piles of insulating neoprene and rot. I try to force away an unthinkable solution to Sully's condition.

"How did you get here?" I ask him.

It's amazing Sully survived the attack at all. That he made the deep dive and ascent into this cave without scuba is even more astounding. But I remember he stayed underwater looking for my mask so long that everyone but Jake began to worry. Sully is a tough man. He's a survivor.

I place my hand on his shoulder, and he lifts his head weakly. "I fought them," He croaks. "I wouldn't let them take me."

"Hush, don't try to speak. You're here now. You're alive."

"Something grabbed me. Like a rocket." His head wobbles around and his words are garbled, but he's determined to tell his story. "It carried me on the surface. I couldn't see it. I wasn't all there. In and out. Fading. It dragged me down. That's all I know. I didn't see it."

He closes his eyes and curls himself up tighter. He asks me nothing about how I got here, where we are. He doesn't even look around. He is in bad shape. I worry he will not last long like this.

*

The bones are pliable, softer than I expect. They're held together by sinewy tendons and lingering threads of shrunken skin and dry muscle. I have to stop to retch at least a half-dozen times as I cut and peel away the brittle wetsuit. I force myself not to think of these fragments that won't let go as the last tenacious bits of a man. Did he die here alone, or were any of these other dead divers alive when he took his last breath? Did they cling to their last moments of life huddled together, cold? Knowing their bodies would never be found?

I feel the presence of these faceless divers hovering over us. "Thank you," I whisper to the pile of their bones, now covered in vomit. "Thank you," I say, looking at the empty dive belt that held the knife I have been using. The Commission insignia is branded into the knife handle. Commission logos emblazoned on the tanks and wetsuits identify the corpses around me. They tell me very little about what these divers were doing, or how they ended up here. But the fact that Ra'Ook brought Sully and me here says more than I want to know about him and his people.

I carry the wetsuit to the water, rinse it as best I can, and place it around Sully's quivering body. I don't have the energy to get another one, but I will have to warm myself soon. For now, I sidle up next to Sully. And for the first time in what may be years, I cry out loud.

When there are no more tears, I prepare myself for the struggle of securing a wetsuit for myself. I explore a little more around the cave. It's like a museum of diving gear; some of it must be almost first generation scuba gear. Some of it could have been used last year. Amidst all of the gear in this cave, I can't find the thing I want most. A flashlight with working batteries.

A drysuit sits propped against a twin-tank rig with extra regulators hanging from it—the uniform of a typical cave diver who plans to go deep and stay long. What's left of the man inside slips out easily once I unzip the baggy drysuit.

There is nothing left inside me. Gagging brings nothing up. I rinse the suit thoroughly, and as I squeeze my head through the rubber neck seal, I recognize the parched feeling of thirst. I glance over at Sully. His lips are dry and cracked. I go back to the stream flowing from the dark corner of the cave and find that it's fresh and tastes clear.

My mask is gone. Fallen into the water when I dragged Sully up. My options are grim, but my only concern now is survival. I rip a mask from the nearest skull and rinse it until I can no longer stand the thirst. I fill it completely and gulp it down. I force Sully to drink some, too. I have propped him against a wall of the cave, and what little body heat he has is being held close to his skin by the wetsuit. I have to get a drysuit for him, too. The two together will warm him.

My dive computer says we have been here five hours. Sully is weak and still shivering. He periodically breaks into fits of convulsive coughing. But he has recovered enough to speak. He tells me he's sorry he didn't save me when I was in the water. "I tried to shoot it, but I didn't want to hit you," he says.

"What do you know about them?" I ask.

Sully looks surprised. "I know they're dangerous."

"You have to tell me what you know," I urge him. "I don't care if you're Commission, Sully. That doesn't matter now."

"I'm not Commission," he says between coughs. "I'm a navy man, young lady. I get my orders straight from the top."

While he coughs and catches his breath, I try to decipher what he means by "the top."

"The navy commander met with me himself before we left," Sully continues. "Told me about those hybrids out there. Guillermo's perrorap are vicious animals—trainable weapons. Dirk thinks the navy's dolphins are impressive? He doesn't know squat. The Commission's got animal experiments crawling all over the blackout zone."

"What did the navy want you to do with them?" I ask him.

"Stay away from 'em, and keep us all safe," he says. "They didn't want trouble with the Commission."

Sully closes his eyes and wipes his mouth. "I'm sorry you ended up here, sweetie. We were almost home safe." He slumps against the wall. The conversation has drained him.

In the corner, the grayness above is growing brighter. I sit beneath it, drifting off into sleep and then waking with a gnawing hunger. Gray turns into blue sky. An opening. Occasionally, I hear a hiss and see the spray from waves crashing somewhere out there.

I'm desperate to reach it. Luminescent slime coats my hands as I try again to climb my way up the smooth, slick walls of the cave. There is no use trying. I have to build something to stand on. I begin stacking scuba tanks against the wall. Then I tell myself that all of this. . . rubble around me is nothing more than rocks and fallen stalactites. Inanimate objects. Dragging them to the corner, I begin to build a pile. Rolling and hoisting them on top of one another. It's exhausting, sweaty work. I have given Sully my drysuit, cutting away the neck seal and wrapping it around him like a jacket. The light above is now clearly sunshine.

My mound is barely five feet tall. From the top of my pile of gear and bones, the fresh air above is no closer. All this work has gained me nothing. It feels like a stupid idea now. My hope sinks, but I hold onto the faint possibility that Ra'Ook will return. That he understands what happened was an accident. It's not what it looked like. I didn't know Sully would shoot at him. But the longer I wait, the more I have to accept reality. There is only one way out of here.

Until now, going down has not seemed like an option. But staying in this tomb can lead to only one outcome. The water may be our only chance for survival. I rehearse it in my mind first. Plan each step. I'll have to find a tank with some air in it for Sully. A regulator. Fins. The wetsuit and drysuit I've draped over him have been cut to fit around him. I'll need to actually wrestle him into a suit for our dive. He is so cold now, he will have no chance of surviving without one.

I check Sully's dive watch. It's almost five. It's been seventeen hours since I left the *Sun Joule* thinking I could save the world with a tablet full of pictures and news stories. Maybe it could have worked, but in this dank echoey cave, our plan seems naïve and silly.

I don't know if my plan to save Sully and myself will work, now. What I do know is that I feel very small and alone.

CHAPTER 23

ASSEMBLING THE GEAR IS PAINFULLY SLOW WORK. WHAT little light spilled into the cave from above is gone now. In the dim light of glowworms and slime, it's difficult to tell, but Sully looks even paler. His raspy breathing concerns me. If he inhaled seawater into his lungs, they may be swelling, drowning him in his own fluids. Worse, the gash in his side may have pierced a lung. He desperately needs medical attention.

I rouse him and tell him it's time to leave. He struggles to sit up away from the wall. As I help him hobble on hands and knees to the water's edge, I realize just how difficult this is going to be. We'll need to hold each other through the whole dive and keep eye contact the way Dirk did with me. I may have to swim us both to the surface. And I don't know what we'll find outside this cave. There may be an island above us, or merely an outcrop of reef. Either way, the crashing waves may pummel us to shreds before we make it to whatever dry land there is up there. Then again, the cave may not open directly beneath us. It might lead us far from here where there would be nothing to do but drift on the open ocean. That is if we even make it out. Below us may be a maze of tunnels to navigate in complete blackness. My lungs spasm reflexively just thinking about my scuba tank running out of air. Pulling in hard for a breath and getting nothing. How long does it take to suffocate?

Something else concerns me more than these scenarios, however. It's the nagging question in the back of my mind. Why did so many trained Commission divers choose death in this cave over trying to dive their way out? What could be waiting for us below?

Sully and I finally reach the collection of gear I have set up. When, the water breaks I jump back, letting go of Sully who slumps to the ground. Ra'Ook surfaces with both hands up, palms facing forward. My heart jumps with a rush of adrenalin. Another man like Ra'Ook breaks the water beside him. His face is larger than Ra'Ook's and rounder with a thicker ridge and longer, deeper slits above his eyes. His shoulders are broader, his chest whiter. I know right away, this is his father.

Sully lunges forward in a burst of energy I didn't know he had. He looks ready to attack. He's too weak to stand, but I slam him back with more force than I intended. "Sully, don't," I order. "If you want to live, let me do this." Stunned, he doesn't put up a fight.

"I'm sorry," Ra'Ook says to me. Relief washes over me. Ra'Ook understands. He believes me. He's taking us back to the boat. "We saw everything," he says. "My father has been in council with his advisors."

ShaOhm raises his hand to stop Ra'Ook from speaking. The backs of his hands and arms are dark. A velvety emerald that looks almost black.

"How do you make this?" he asks me, holding up the tablet.

"Whoa," Sully gurgles propping himself back up with his arm. The effort takes a toll on him, and it shows.

"I don't know," I answer. "It's complicated. But it's what we use to do our work, sort of."

ShaOhm turns the tablet on and pulls up a research paper of Lacey's. It's all text. "What is this?" he asks me.

I read Lacey's paper out loud. I'm barely through the abstract when ShaOhm stops me and points to the screen. "I don't understand these symbols. Why do you bring them to me?"

The battery on the tablet has to be almost dead. I quickly click over to her music file and play a song. There is no video on the screen. Just M.T. Banks' cover of the Beatles "Money can't buy you love."

Ra'Ook and his father watch the blank screen and then look up at each other. "Some of this isn't for you," I say. "It's for us. We have these devices for ourselves. It's entertainment, and it's how we communicate around the world. It was all I had to show you."

The two of them speak to each other in their language, and it sounds like cellos playing a haunting duet. Sully has slumped back down and is lying on his side, moaning slightly. I think he is praying. I gently rub my hand across his shoulder.

"It's OK, Sully. They're not from the Commission," I whisper. "They're a different species. The Commission is keeping them a secret."

"No," he says. There is such fear in his face. "The Commission trains hybrids. They're hideous."

Sully coughs so hard, he spits blood. Ra'Ook and his father look over at us.

"If what you show me is true," ShaOhm says, "your black death is a stupid mistake, and your people are children who follow blindly the leaders who lie to them." The disgust in his thunderous voice fills the cave. We hadn't meant for the videos to make us look weak and stupid. He doesn't understand the whole thing.

"The people you negotiate with are not our leaders," I tell him. "I think I know who they are. They are here on these islands, right?"

"Yes. When we meet, they come here from many shores. We make our treaties here."

"That's got to be the Commission. They don't represent us," I insist. "Most of the world doesn't know about you. If they did, they would help. They would stop destroying your oceans. Everything would change." As I say it, the vision of Sully standing at the stern with his spear gun pointed at Ra'Ook sticks in my head. Some people would help the Mers. Some would want to kill them. Even Jake said Ra'Ook belonged in an aquarium. He didn't mean it. He was mad, and scared, but the thought matters. It wasn't very long ago when European explorers put native Alaskans and Africans on exhibit at fairs and circuses. They kept them in cages. People. Human beings. Maybe society has moved beyond that. But despite all their humanity, ShaOhm and his people are not human beings. I am afraid the world would not be as eager to help them as I said they would.

ShaOhm studies my face. He looks at Sully breathing in raspy gulps. "We cease the attack for now," he says sternly. "We will remove the black crust."

My chin sinks to my chest. "Thank you."

"Another accident with the black death will not be tolerated. If you have lied, there will be no mercy. Nothing but our Fouling, as you call it, will live on your shores again."

The cease fire is temporary, and I am both relieved and horrified.

"We now go back to your home," Ra'Ook says, extending his hand to me.

"NO!" his father booms, his face flashing white and red

186

as his voice echoes through the cave. "No returning. They have seen too much. Especially this one," he says, pointing to me. He speaks English for me. So I will understand.

Ra'Ook shrinks away from me. He puts his hands up to face me. His father can see, but shows no recognition. It's clear now that this sign of friendship is ours alone. "Can I say goodbye?" Ra'Ook asks him, again in English. ShaOhm juts his head forward and makes a high-pitched whistle. Then he flicks his hand up toward me. I think he's disgusted.

Ra'Ook swims closer. I lean over the edge. Sully rolls forward weakly to grab me, but misses. Ra'Ook's hands touch mine. I bend my head toward his and our foreheads rest against one another. Ra'Ook closes his eyes and whispers, "Trust RahEee."

In an instant, they're gone. I stare into the black water for a long time after they leave.

Sully coughs behind me. He lies on his side, his hands trembling in front of his face. He looks old and weak. His eyes are barely open. I drape my arm over his shoulder. He is so cold.

"I didn't know," he repeats over and over, so softly I can barely hear him.

"The Commission experiments were a myth," I tell him. "Barru Pi's craziness, her weapons, all lies. Even the Commission is a lie Sully. They aren't here to clean up the islands. They're here to keep the Merpeople secret. Government leaders around the world must know about everything. They've distracted us with myths all this time. No one ever looked for the truth, Sully."

Sully has stopped shaking. His breathing is shallow and raspy. Exhausted, I let myself lie down next to him. "Trust RahEee," Ra'Ook said. I repeat it to myself, hoping that will help me understand what he meant. "Trust RahEee." I just need rest so I can think clearly.

I wake with Sully rustling fitfully next to me. "Julie?" he says, "Julie, don't let go." His eyes open and he leans toward me. "Hold on, baby girl, I gotcha."

"Sully, it's me, Alannis."

He no longer shivers. Through his groggy mumbling, he tries to roll his head up to look at me. I scooch closer and lay his head in my lap. "I'm holding on," I say, scared that he doesn't see me. He sees her. But somehow his words comfort me anyway.

"I've got you," he mumbles. Please stay with me, Sully.

For a long time, he seems to sleep. I can't feel his pulse, but I keep my hand on his chest to feel the small rise and fall of his breathing. Minutes go by, maybe hours. The faint pulse of waves drones somewhere outside of here. A distant rhythm. *Crushhhh, whooshhh, pssshhh.* It feels good to let it take over. So quiet, *crushhhh, whooshhh,* pssshhh. I could sleep now. Rest a while with Sully until he is better. He might get better.

I watch the reflection of twinkling glowworms ripple out from the center of the black water in front of us. Hours, days. I don't know. Gradually, I become aware that these ripples mean something is moving below. A small dome of black hair emerges from the ripples. RahEee's head appears, her eyes big and excited. "Gkaoum," she says smiling with what looks like pride. She sounds like a gourd drum that changes pitch with each beat. She says it a few more times before I realize she is saying "Come."

"Al' anss, Gkaoum," she says. I have to believe in Ra'Ook. Trust RahEee. The water is our only way out. I slip my legs from beneath Sully's head and begin to gather our gear. RahEee clicks and points at Sully then sweeps her arm to the side. "Gno," she says. "Gno."

Sully can't go. RahEee is not strong enough for both of us, and Sully is not strong enough to survive the dive.

I feel the presence of decades' worth of dead bodies all around me. The man in my arms is wrapped in the wetsuit of someone else who took his last breath in this crypt. We can't die here with them.

RahEee urges me to come now. I can't leave him to die alone. Leave his body here with these anonymous others. RahEee clicks loudly and slaps the water. I have to make a decision.

I remember the wretched smell of death when I first arrived in this cave. It has grown faint, and doesn't bother me now. My nose has adjusted.

I don't have to die here. I won't die here. I grab the knife I have been using and scratch Sully's name and the year into the soft rock floor beside him. I can't remember his first name. Jack. Jacob. Jerry, maybe. I don't want to get it wrong. So, I write "Captain Sully Sullivan." There is nothing more I can do for him.

I pull a mask from the pile. Don the rest of my gear. I hold his hand and slide myself into the water. He opens his eyes. They're dull and glassy, but they watch me. His hand twitches slightly. He wants to reach for me. I lift it to my face, so much heavier than I expected.

"Julie. My sunshine." It's barely a whisper.

I'm hit with a vision of my father. I press Sully's hand to my cheek. I want so badly to see my father again. And to give Sully something before I leave him. "I'm here Daddy. I'm right here with you." I brush wisps of white hair from his forehead. Press my lips to his cheek. "I love you, Daddy. Be brave."

RahEee wraps her hand around my arm and pulls me

down. Right before I submerge, Sully's blue eyes fill with recognition and fear. "I'll be back, Daddy." Another lie among so many.

Through the pitch black, I feel RahEee guiding me. Blind twists and turns confuse our descent. I would never have found my way out, or back to the cave. I wonder how many more dead bodies are resting in the water here. Those who chose escape. Sully and I didn't have a chance on our own. I tell myself over and over that he didn't have a chance anyway. But every turn we make feels like another key locking him in. I should have begged RahEee harder.

When we reach fresh air, we're far from the sound of waves. RahEee wraps my hands around her shoulders and swims with me. She is so much smaller than Ra'Ook, but she is strong and her swimming is just as steady and graceful. We stop to rest. My tank is nearly empty, so we travel on the surface until I see a spot light sweeping the water in the distance. I can't believe they're still out here. They're looking for me!

RahEee dives below and within minutes, we surface right in the path of the blinding white searchlight. It will be over me in seconds, but my head will be barely visible to them. Before I can wave my arms and shout out, RahEee touches my chest. She holds her two hands up, palms facing me. "Ra'Ook," she says, and then points to the boat. "Al 'anns. Sss 'Afe."

Ra'Ook told her to do this. To bring me to my boat, make sure I was safe. I trusted him, and he has kept me safe. I touch her shoulder and say, "Thank you, RahEee." I don't know if she knows the words, it doesn't matter. Rescue is the only thing on my mind now.

The light sweeps over me. I call out for help, but the minute I hear my own voice, a horrible sound registers. A sound that, until now, was overpowered by excitement. The rumbling of an engine. RahEee made a mistake. This is not the *Sun Joule*.

Voices call out, and the light locks onto me. RahEee is gone. The angle of the light is low to the water, obscuring the boat. Closer than I thought. It's small. An inflatable. As it comes up beside me, someone reaches a hand over. I recognize the silver and black uniform of the Commission.

CHAPTER 24

MY RESCUERS HAUL ME ABOARD, AND WE TAKE OFF TO-
ward a red beacon in the distance. When we reach the
submarine, they urge me up the ladder onto the deck. One of
them leads me into a dark control room. "We are overjoyed
that you have survived your ordeal," a stern officer says and
introduces himself to me as Lieutenant Reese. He wraps a
scratchy wool blanket around my shoulders, and offers me a
large mug of hot tea. I am told to sit. The only chairs are the
swivel kind bolted to the floor. They're lined up in front of a
bank of lights and monitors. A uniformed woman approaches
me with a medical bag. She takes my temperature, blood
pressure, and pulse. She looks in my eyes, asks me to squeeze
her hands. When she's done, she nods at the lieutenant and
leaves.

"Your shipmates tell a gruesome tale of your demise," Lt.
Reese says, pacing around the control bridge. "One of them,
Lacey is it? Traumatized. The poor girl imagines you were
carried away in the jaws of a monstrous creature."

Lieutenant Reese leans over me and places his hands on
the armrests of my chair. "How lucky you are that we found
you. And without a single scratch." He continues to marvel out
loud about my chances of surviving an attack, of drifting all
day and night, and most remarkable of all, being found. He
asks me no questions.

Another man enters with two plates of eggs and sausage. He sets them at the control station beside me. "Hello Alannis. I'm Commander Talbot. Sorry I took so long in getting to you." My stomach aches from hunger. Butter melts into a steaming biscuit on the side of each plate. He looks me up and down and then barks an order. "Reese, what are you thinking? This child is still wet and cold. Take her to Perez."

I think I'm going to pass out as Lt. Reese leads me away from the smell of those warm biscuits and sweet sausages. He takes me to a small cabin where a woman named Officer Perez hands me Commission sweat pants and a shirt and shows me to a hot shower. When I'm finished, she returns me to Captain Talbot.

He immediately places the plate of food in front of me. "Eat, please."

While I shovel eggs and biscuit into my mouth, Commander Talbot sits back in the chair next to mine. "You must be exhausted. Why don't you tell me everything you've been through," he says, "then you can go get some rest."

"I don't know what happened," I insist between bites.

Of course, that's not what he wants to hear. Long after I've finished eating, he's still pressing me to answer him. For all his feigned concern, he's not about to let me rest yet.

My answers are always the same.

"It was dark."

"I was too scared to see anything."

"I can't remember."

"I must have blacked out."

Eventually, Perez takes me back to the cabin. I'm allowed to sleep. I dream of Sully. Still lingering, alone and cold, calling me, begging me not to leave him. I awaken screaming his name with Perez shaking my shoulders. She does her best to comfort me and act sisterly. All the while she tries to coax me into telling her about my nightmare.

*

From what I can tell, I've been aboard this submarine for three days. Lt. Reese and Commander Talbot grill me tag team style. Reese is harsh and threatening. Talbot is fatherly and sickeningly sweet. Their questions are mostly monotonous repetition. How did I survive my "shark" attack? Who was downloading information the night before I disappeared? Why was a member of the science team so worried about me in the beginning of the trip? Am I hiding something?

They're relentless. I'm starting to cave.

I have to tell them something. I can't go on like this. I try to think strategically. What can I give them? Then something so obvious occurs to me that I can't believe I didn't think of it sooner.

"I did see something," I tell Lt. Reese who raises his eyebrows and swivels his chair to face mine.

"I saw the Fouling on the first day when I was swimming. Snorkeling actually."

I try to think quickly. If Ra'Ook told us the truth, I can lead the Commission to the bacteria that stops the Fouling. "There wasn't a lot of Fouling, and there was something that looked like algae all over it, especially around the edges." I hope I sound convincing as I imagine what it looks like.

"That's quite a secret to keep for so long," Lt. Reese says. "Wasn't that the main goal of the trip? To find the Fouling?"

"I was afraid to tell anyone because I was snorkeling in a blackout zone. The Fouling was on a shipwreck. I thought I would get in trouble for seeing it."

"I'm glad you're beginning to trust me," he says.

For what feels like hours, he makes me tell him what I

saw, why I was there, how we got there. He asks me the same questions a dozen different ways, and I struggle to keep track of my lies. Eventually, I also tell him I'm responsible for the big download the night before I disappeared. I stick with the story I suggested to Jake and Candace. Last minute effort to do a school project about my trip. He never takes his eyes off of me. He never blinks. When he stands up to pace around the control room, I'm relieved that he's not staring at me.

"You have quite a survival instinct," he says, walking behind me, out of view. "You are a puzzle, though." I drop my eyes and focus on my hands while he pauses and drums his fingers on a counter somewhere. "When I think about the night of your attack, well, it's curious to me that such a smart girl would leave her boat in the middle of the night to go diving alone in the first place."

Lt. Reese reaches over my shoulder from behind and places a scuba mask on the control desk in front of me. My heart stops for two full beats. It's the mask I wore when they rescued me. The old-style Commission mask I pulled from the pile in the cave. Instantly, I know what this means. I fight the urge to run. I tell myself to breath and not panic. But the mask in front of me feels like a fire burning out of control.

"You have an interesting sense of style, Miss Summers," Lt. Reese says. When he walks around to face me, I'm surprised he's smiling. "I'm not going to ask you why you went diving. Or where you ended up. I know you won't tell me. You are very good at keeping secrets, aren't you?"

My hands tremble. My heart beats like a grounded fish trying to flap its way back to the water. I stare at a bank of monitors across from me. If he wants to know where I was, or how to find the Mers, I won't tell him. I couldn't even if I wanted to, because I don't know where I was.

"Do you believe in the Triad, Miss Summers?" His tightlipped laugh sounds more like a cough. "Of course you do. You believe in mysterious things lurking underwater. Things that would be difficult to explain. And you do understand the importance of our work here on Cubbarros, don't you?"

"Yes." I squeeze the word out. But suddenly, something inside me shifts, a sudden acceptance of fate. I am beyond the point of fear. If they want to torture me, kill me, I can't stop them. I just want this to be over. "No, actually," I argue, "I don't even know for sure what your work is on Cubbarros. Can you just tell me that? Can you tell me what we're all doing here?"

"Well, *you're* here because you've been making friends in a dangerous neighborhood." He waits for me to flinch. I have no doubt now, he knows what I've seen. My face settles into stone.

"So, I'm friendly," I sneer back at him.

"Yes, well, that's a valuable trait, the ability to make friends. And now, we have to decide just how valuable it is, Miss Summers, because we're here to keep people out of dangerous neighborhoods. And, most importantly, to contain the danger." To contain ShaOhm and his people is what he really means, but he won't say it.

"The only thing dangerous in these waters is secrecy." I scowl. "If people were nicer, maybe it would be a better neighborhood. Maybe everyone should learn to get along."

"For a smart girl, you're very naïve," he chuckles and shakes his head. "Secrets keep your lovely little world from turning itself inside out. We are a society dependant on international trade, Miss Summers. He who controls the oceans controls the power. Do you think people are prepared

196

to share that?" Reese sits down across from me and glides his fingers around the mask as he speaks. "Mankind stands alone on this Earth. Thinking, reasoning, speaking. Try taking that away from people."

Lt. Reese motions for me to stand up and leave the room. Perez waits by the door to escort me back to our cabin. Is that it? They can't be finished with me. Perez hands me black cargo pants and a t-shirt to change into. What's coming next? Will I be tortured for more information? Or are they going to kill me to keep their secret from getting out?

Then Perez directs me to a ladder leading up to an open hatch. For the first time in days my eyes squint into a blue sky. Fresh air. But I'm reluctant to go. This is what it must feel like to be led to the gallows.

As my head emerges from the hatch, Commander Talbot is there on deck to give me a hand up. "I'm glad we finally understand each other," he says, although I don't understand anything. Two officers are assembling an inflatable boat on the deck of this submarine. I assume they're my hangmen, preparing to oversee my death. A deep lonely plunge to the bottom of the ocean, perhaps. My knees buckle. I crumble inside. I'm ready to tell Commander Talbot whatever he wants to know. I just don't know what that is exactly.

"What do you want me to do?" I ask him.

"You have already done what no one else has," he says. I watch the men ease the boat down the curved deck of the sub. "You have survived out here," he pauses to study my face, "without our protection."

"So far," I say in a small defeated voice.

"Exactly! And you would do it again if we asked you to, wouldn't you?"

"Yes." It's the answer he wants, but I don't understand

what he means. Are they taking me back to the cave?

"The Commission needs someone. . . friendly. Like you," he says, putting his hand heavily on my shoulder. "Someone with friends who trust them. Yes, that would be very valuable to us, indeed."

"You want me to work for you?" I ask incredulously.

"Oh, not right away. Let's let things die down a little. You go back to your studies. Marine biology, isn't it?"

I'm not sure what to say. They want to use my friendship with Ra'Ook to groom me for a position in the Commission? I stare at the heat waves radiating from the dark surface of the sub. The sea is flat, not a whisper of air moves.

"It's your choice," he says. "Of course you can say no. But enough of that for now. Let's get you back to your boat." He places his hand between my shoulder blades and guides me across the deck. "Given how touch and go your condition was over these past few days, they will be glad to hear you have pulled through." I can't imagine what they told the team on the *Sun Joule*, but I don't want to think about just how touch and go it was.

As the inflatable's engine comes to life, Commander Talbot helps me down into the small boat. "You're a very lucky young lady," he says, pressing something into my hand. "Just between us, I trust you will make the right choices for your future."

The boat speeds away, and hot air blasts my face. I uncurl my fingers to find the shark's tooth anklet that I placed on my dresser before I left home. His message is crystal clear. I can't escape this. There is only one choice if I am to have any future at all. My hair whips around into a tangled mess as I scan the horizon. Nothing but white flat-bottomed clouds. The *Sun Joule* must be miles away.

CHAPTER 25

WE REACH THE *SUN JOULE* IN THE EARLY AFTERNOON. I'M
numb from the drone of the motor and the constant pounding
of the small boat against the sea. The team stands on deck,
calling my name. They hover over me as I climb aboard. They
thought I would never make it back. Jake pushes through them
and wraps his arms around me. I'm overcome by a feeling of
security. He has me. It feels like I've been struggling to hold
everything together for so long. With his embrace, I can let go
now.

Jake releases me. His crystal blue eyes are unmistakably
Sully's. I bury my face in his chest. "He's gone," I cry.

"I know," Jake responds, "Lacey saw it. We all know. It's
not your fault."

I can't tell him. How could I? No one will ever
understand why I left his father to die. Why I saved myself and
left him there alone. Would I have done the same thing if it
had been my father? I don't think I could have. I don't know
any more what I did or why I did it. It's something no one will
ever understand, because they weren't there. I can't tell another
soul. It's something I will live with for the rest of my life.

"He's gone," I whisper.

Jake's arms tighten around my shoulders. He rests his
cheek on the top of my head, and holds me close to his chest.
He moves one hand to my head, slides his fingers through my

hair, clenches them into a fist and squeezes me hard in his arms, trying not to cry. I can feel him struggling to steady his breath, gather his strength. He's trying to be stoic, burying his grief for now the way Sully would have wanted.

When he loosens his arms, I don't want to look up. I don't want to see his father's eyes again, but he lifts my chin gently. "I'm glad you're here," he says, "and you're alive." He leans down toward me. Our eyes fix on each other and our lips meet. His kiss is soft and easy. Then he closes his eyes and kisses me with the full force of his relief. I survived. I came back alive.

My arms wrap around him as if I'll never let go.

Candace puts her hand on my shoulder. "It's stopped," she says, turning me around to face her. "The Fouling has not progressed for the past three days." ShaOhm kept his promise.

"We've been on the Satellite phone," Jake tells me. "They've been sending updates."

"It's self-limiting," Lacey adds. "It only lasts so long, and then it dies back, like a red tide, or a swarm of locusts. It's already begun receding in some places."

Jake and Candace give me a knowing look. Then Candace asks me to sit down. "We had to tell your parents," she says. "They've been in Florida trying to convince the navy to send out search planes." My parents. What they must be going through. Adrenalin rushes through me.

"We have to call them," I shout.

"Our sat connection was blocked this morning," Candace says. "The navy is sending a boat for you. They want to talk with you."

"No way. Not again. I want to go home." I look at Jake. "Please, take me home."

*

200

Another long ride in a small inflatable, and it's pitch black outside by the time I reach the navy submarine. I'm sickened by claustrophobia as we enter through the hatch. I can't do this. They take me to a room with white walls and a small conference table bolted to the floor. There's a chart on the wall with rollers above it for what looks like a movie screen and a half dozen other charts. A man in a marine uniform tells me to sit, and the ship's commander begins questioning me. What did the Commission want from me? What did the submarine look like? Do I remember the layout, or anything about the controls? His voice is light and compassionate. He doesn't treat me like an enemy.

The marine officer brings me coffee, which I don't like. But it's going to be a long night. I load it with sugar that doesn't quite mask its bitterness. I force it down anyway. They apologize for keeping me up and tell me they want to get me back to my boat as quickly as possible. Then the commander begins with the big questions. What happened out there? What attacked you? Was it big? Was it a sea lion? Did it bring you straight to the Commission sub? Was the Commission giving it orders? Did the Commission tell you anything about it?

He believes what Sully believed. That the Commission is training animals as military spies and weapons. This guy definitely doesn't suspect me of anything. It's almost as if I'm some kind of hero—a hardworking research assistant bravely seeking a solution to the Fouling who was attacked by the Commission's trained animals. I tell him I was too scared and weak and delirious to know what was going on. He appears to be utterly convinced.

A loud drumming echoes through the steel submarine. "The helicopter's here," the marine says. He steps outside the room. A few minutes pass, and a man walks in wearing a black

201

suit with a crisp white shirt and a red tie. He looks immensely out of place, and very hot.

He extends his hand to shake mine. "James Perry, Secretary of Defense," he says. This is serious business. The only person above him is the president. He controls the whole military. I'm so glad to see him. I can tell him everything about the Commission. What they want. What they're hiding. He could go to the president, and they could take care of it. If anyone could keep me safe, it's these guys.

Mr. Perry asks the commander to give us a few minutes alone, and then sits across from me. He interlaces his fingers in front of him. "So, I want to extend our deepest concerns for your safety and our relief that you're OK."

"Thank you," I answer.

"I know you want to get home, so I won't keep you. I am here to convey to you the president's sincere concern for what you have endured, and to express our appreciation. To thank you, Miss Summers."

He pauses and waits for me to ask, "Thank me for what?"

"For your honesty. The Fouling crisis seems to be coming to an end. But knowing where to find a controlling agent is very, very important in helping us prevent it in the future."

He watches the recognition register on my face. I told the Commission to look for the control on the shipwreck.

"It would probably have been better if you had disclosed that information when you first discovered it. Maybe none of this would have happened. But I understand. You were afraid." His voice is terrifyingly pleasant and unthreatening.

"I thought it best for me to come here and let you know in person. There is nothing to be afraid of. We're all on the same team, after all."

My stomach drops. My head spins. This is the most

frightening thing I've ever heard. The Commission and the secretary of defense. On the same team. The president!

"How big is the team?" I ask, half hoping he doesn't answer.

"The ones who know what we know? Small. You've already met some of our officers. Beyond that, just the key leaders who set up the Commission. Presidents, prime ministers, a few kings. You're in very rare company, dear." The Secretary of Defense stands and opens the door.

A marine officer in dress uniform escorts Mr. Perry and me to the deck, and they both climb into the waiting helicopter. The wind and rotor spray settle as they disappear into the early morning sky. It's that kind of cobalt blue sky that's just about to explode into gold. I used to love the moments right before sunrise, so full of potential for the day ahead.

The uniformed marine guides me to the boat that will take me back to the *Sun Joule*. He nods his head at me respectfully. "That was some honor, there. We're proud to have had you aboard, Miss Summers." He doesn't have a clue who he's really serving, or why.

*

When we finally get close enough, I recognize Dirk on the bow. He's waiting to haul the anchor up. No one wants to stay here any longer than we have to. The navy guys give me a little salute when they shove off and head back to their submarine.

Within minutes, the *Sun Joule* is on her way home. I sink down onto a bench seat on the lower deck and let my eyes close.

It's nearly noon when I wake up. Lacey and Dirk are making fruit smoothies in the galley. Lacey hands me one, and Matt comes upstairs from the lab. He tells me the bacteria Jake

203

showed him appear to consume the Fouling. "We can't say for sure until we run more experiments," he clarifies. "This work is going to last quite a while, but Candace is including Jake's name on the research paper."

She better. He knew it all along. I'm glad for Jake. It can't erase what he's going through, but it's something worth going home to. With his name on a research paper, and Candace in his corner, he'll get back to school. She'll make sure he gets his degree.

Guillermo walks in looking at me as if I've returned from the dead. "Ah, I thought I heard your lovely voice." He squeezes my shoulders and gives me a peck on the cheek. His cigar is burning away, filling the salon with its thick sweet smoke. He points it at Lacey and Dirk. "You understand, now, yes? There is truth in my stories."

"What was it like?" Matt asks me. "The perrorap? Lacey said it was just like Guillermo described."

"I didn't see it," I tell them. "I must have passed out. Do you mind if we don't talk about it?"

Dirk says our satellite connection is back, and Candace is trying to raise my parents on the sat phone. She's in the wheelhouse with Jake. I make my way to the upper deck where I can see them behind the door. I'll have to tell them about meeting ShaOhm. But I'm not ready to talk about any of it right now. I can't wait to hear my parents' voices. I imagine running down the dock into their arms. The three of us, holding each other. Will Jake's mother be there? Waiting for her son to run down the dock, to hold her up? This is all so unfair.

*

Watching Jake through the glass, Sully's voice haunts me. "I've gotcha," he repeats over and over. I'm ashamed of what I did, even if it was necessary. But I can't change it. I feel guilty and sorry for myself at the same time. The Commission weighs on my shoulders. What lies ahead for me?

A white, foamy wake spreads out behind the back of our boat. This ship is just a tiny dot in the middle of a huge ocean. There is so much we don't understand. When I met Ra'Ook, I fantasized that I had discovered him. That I would be the one to bring his story to light. Now, instead, I will be forced to help hide his existence. I'm a part of the conspiracy.

My future scares me, and I'm filled with dread for the day the Commission calls. And yet, buried in all of the horror, I'm sickened and ashamed to find a twinge of excitement. I know I will see Ra'Ook again. And I can't help but have a small bit of hope that, together, maybe we can change things.

Restricted Waters is being used in classrooms to foster discussions about topics relevant to Language Arts, Social Studies, the Environment and Marine Sciences. Below is a sample of questions from the free classroom guide for teachers.

To download the free classroom guide, or to learn about author visits and virtual classroom sessions,
visit **RestrictedWaters.com**

SAMPLE DISCUSSION QUESTIONS

1] Describe Alannis's relationship with Jake, Candace, and Sully. What aspect of her personality does each relationship reveal? How do these relationships change during the expedition?

2] How does Alannis's background influence her desire to join the expedition? Why does she feel she needs to prove herself to the scientific team?

3] When Alannis believes Jake is jealous that she is exploring with Ra'Ook, Jake snaps at her, "Jealous? Of what, your fishboy?" What does his choice of words imply about Alannis's feelings for Ra'Ook? About Jake's feelings for her? What does his use of the word "fishboy" say about Jake's attitude toward Ra'Ook?

4] English writer William Hazlitt said "Prejudice is the child of ignorance." What does he mean? What role does ignorance play in Jake's feelings toward Ra'Ook? What about fear? Jealousy?

5)   The Fouling was planted by the Mers, but it spread rapidly in its new environment until it covered everything. Why didn't it do the same in the Cubbarros Islands? What role did petroleum oil and bacteria play in the ability of the Fouling to invade coastal towns?

6)   Explain why the Commission wants to keep the Mers a secret? What do you think might happen if people knew about the Mers? Would it change the way people view their own place in the world? Would all people accept the Mers?

7)   Do you think the Commission is afraid of the Mers in some way? What evidence does the author give for this?

8)   Can you describe any parallels between the Mer's experience with humans and cultural events in history? Provide examples. Explain similarities and differences?

9)   Why do Ra'Ook and Sha'Ohm think people have been attacking the Mers? How might human activity look like an attack to someone living in the ocean?

10) Alannis tells Sha'Ohm that if people knew about Mers. ". . .They would stop destroying your oceans. Everything would change." Does Alannis believe that's true? Do you?

11) Scientists have explored only a tiny fraction of the oceans. Can you explain why? What technological obstacles do ocean explorers face?

12) What does it mean when the color of Ra'Ook and Sha'Ohm's skin shifts from blue to red or orange? What real-life animals change color to communicate emotions? Did you include humans?

Kara Lynn Conyer

received a B.A. in magazine journalism and a B.A. in anthropology from Syracuse University. After many years as a science writer and a science diver for the Smithsonian Institution, she has learned a few things about what it's like to be on an expedition in the middle of the ocean. When she's not gathering the facts, she likes to imagine what secrets might lie beneath them. *Restricted Waters* is her first novel.

Visit her at RestrictedWaters.com

www.ingramcontent.com/pod-product-compliance
Lightning Source LLC
Chambersburg PA
CBHW050931120626
46552CB00001B/160